Lady Herbert

Abyssinia and its apostle

Lady Herbert

Abyssinia and its apostle

ISBN/EAN: 9783741185441

Manufactured in Europe, USA, Canada, Australia, Japa

Cover: Foto ©Andreas Hilbeck / pixelio.de

Manufactured and distributed by brebook publishing software
(www.brebook.com)

Lady Herbert

Abyssinia and its apostle

ABYSSINIA AND ITS APOSTLE.

BY

LADY HERBERT.

————

LONDON:

BURNS, OATES, & CO., 17, 18 PORTMAN STREET,

AND 63 PATERNOSTER ROW.

TO

THE VERY REV. HERBERT VAUGHAN, D.D.

FOUNDER OF THE MISSIONARY COLLEGE AT MILL HILL,

THIS HUMBLE TRANSLATION

OF

THE LIFE OF ONE

IN WHOSE FOOTSTEPS HE NEEDS

NOT THE WILL, BUT ONLY THE OPPORTUNITY,

TO FOLLOW,

IS AFFECTIONATELY AND RESPECTFULLY INSCRIBED.

PREFACE.

WHEN I began the translation of this little book at the beginning of the year, I only thought of giving my readers the biography of a holy and apostolic Bishop, living in this nineteenth century, with whose reputation for sanctity and wisdom my Eastern wanderings had made me acquainted, even before the French publication of his Life.

Other and more pressing occupations made me lay aside the translation for some months, when I was induced to resume it for the following reasons. Recent political events have given to Abyssinia a fresh interest in the minds of Englishmen ; and, in addition to this, I felt that the accurate descriptions of roads, scenery, and manners, detailed in Mgr. de Jacobis' letters, together with his just appreciation of the character of the Emperor who at present rules over that unfortunate country, might perhaps be of some assistance to those concerned in the present war, and enable them to estimate better the difficulties they will have to encounter, and the character of the man with whom they have to deal.

MARY ELISABETH HERBERT.

Jamaica, December 1, 1867.

CONTENTS.

———

ABYSSINIA AND ITS APOSTLE.

CHAPTER I.

The religious history of Abyssinia—Early life of Mgr. de Jacobis.

ENGLISH people in general have a suspicion and a dislike of any thing which pretends to be the life of a saint. To begin with, the idea runs counter to all their preconceived ideas and prejudices: " There are no saints," they will tell you, " out of the Bible; and as for miracles, they have ceased to exist since the days of the Apostles." We will not enter into the discussion of these points in this little book; and yet we hope to prove to such of our readers as have the patience to follow our story, that, in this nineteenth century of progress, and railroads, and electric wires, and materialism, there yet are men leading lives of devotion and sanctity equal to any in ages of a purer and more unquestioning faith; and that God rewards such lives by manifesting through them His power and glory in a manner utterly unexplainable by human philosophy or natural causes.

But, before entering upon the life of our hero,
we will give some account of the land which was the
theatre of his labours, and of the people for whom
he, six short years ago, laid down his life, after the
example of his great Master.

The country known by the name of Abyssinia
is governed by an Emperor, formerly calling himself
" King of kings;" for his empire extended from
Kaffa, which is close to the Mountains of the Moon,
in the fourth degree of latitude, to the Red Sea.   The
dynasty pretends to have originated with Solomon,
through his son Ménélik, whose mother was the
famous Queen of Sheba.   Her capital was in Arabia
Felix, as many ancient inscriptions prove ; and, hearing of the wisdom of Solomon, she proceeded to Jerusalem, and there was instructed in the Jewish faith.
On her return to her own country, she sent her son
to obtain the same advantages ; and tradition asserts
that Solomon brought him up among his own children.
When he was grown up, and wished to return to
Arabia, Solomon gave him several eminent doctors
of the Church, and priests, to accompany him, at the
head of whom was Azarias, a descendant of Sadok,
in whose race the Levitical succession is still maintained.   They are called " Nebrid," and have the
exclusive right of the priesthood.   Ménélik's dominions extended to Africa, to a portion of which he
gave the name of Ethiopia.   In Holy Writ, the wife

of Moses, who was a Midianite, is likewise called an Ethiopian; for the part of Arabia adjoining Mount Sinai in those times bore that name.

This dynasty of Solomon's—from Ménélik to the eleventh century of the Christian era—reigned supreme in this vast country.

But, about that time, a Jewess, named Judith, indignant at the progress which Christianity had made under the protection of Christian emperors, resolved to upset the existing government, and to place a purely Jewish monarch on the throne. She got possession of the mountain of Devra-Damo, in the country of Tigré, where the imperial family had taken refuge, and massacred all that fell into her hands. Only one boy escaped from the fury of this new Athaliah; who, having established her new kingdom, reigned for forty years. Five Jewish princes succeeded her; but then the Christians again took up arms, and reconquered the throne, which was filled about the year 1200 by a wise and good monarch named Lalibala, who restored and rebuilt the Christian churches, and appointed as his successor the descendant of the boy who had escaped from Judith's wholesale massacre; so that the ancient dynasty was fairly reëstablished in Abyssinia. This last event was brought about by the influence of a holy monk, named Tecla-Haïmanot, who, by his exhortations and his eloquence, induced Lalibala to resign the throne in favour of the lawful heir.

From this time till the seventeenth century, the descendants of Solomon remained undisturbed possessors of the crown; though their power began to be limited by a people called Gallas, from the coast of Zanzibar, and by the incursions of the Mussulman tribes along the borders of the Red Sea. At the time that our English traveller, Bruce, made his first expedition into the country, the reigning emperor was named Tecla-Immanot; but he was more of a monk than a king; and, soon after abandoning the sceptre for a religious state, he was succeeded by his brother, Tecla-Ghiorghis, who was virtually the last emperor: for the commander-in-chief of the Abyssinian army, by a succession of intrigues, got possession of the whole kingdom; and, though he never took the title of emperor, yet, having usurped the whole power, Tecla's reign was at an end, and he was even confined to the precincts of his own palace. The same state of things continues to this day. Mgr. Biancheri, in 1860, writes: " I have seen two of these phantom kings, descendants of Solomon, more than half naked, and dying of hunger, yet still rejoicing in the title of ' Djian-oi'—which means ' your majesty,' and which is the only shadow left them of their past grandeur. Since that, an adventurer named Theodoros has usurped both the power and title of Emperor, and has disarmed the petty princes who had taken possession of different portions of the empire; but his cruelty and tyranny will, probably, make his reign one of short continuance."

After this rapid survey of the political phases through which Abyssinia has passed, we will turn to the question of its religious condition.

"In old times," say the Abyssinians, "our ancestors worshiped the serpent." It was the Queen of Sheba and her son who taught them the knowledge of the true God, and established the Jewish faith among them.

After the death of Christ, they affirm that Christian baptism was introduced among them through the intervention of the eunuch of Queen Candace, who was baptised by St. Philip; but, having no priests to instruct them in the faith, they remained for three centuries in a state hovering between the Old Testament and the New.

About the year 340, Christianity was established in the land, through the apostolic labours of St. Frumentius. His history was a curious one. Born at Tyre, he accompanied his uncle and brother on a voyage of discovery to the coast of Ethiopia; and, on their way home, they touched at a certain port for provisions and fresh water. The barbarians seized the ship, and put every one on board of her to the sword, save Frumentius and his little brother Edesius, who had gone on shore, and were learning their lessons under a tree. Their youth and beauty touched the

hearts of the Ethiopians, who carried them off as
slaves to their king, who resided at Axuma—then a
mighty city, now a miserable village; but filled with
ruins of stately edifices and sumptuous obelisks. The
king was charmed with the children, and took especial
care of their education; making Edesius his cup-bearer,
and intrusting Frumentius, after a few years, with the
gravest concerns of the state.   On his death-bed the
king gave them their liberty; but they remained to
assist the queen-regent in transacting the affairs of the
country; and Frumentius did every thing which lay
in his power to spread the knowledge of Christianity
throughout the empire, establishing several Christian
merchants in the principal towns, and himself setting
an example which attracted all the better class of
infidels to the true faith.   When the new king was of
an age to take the reins of government, the brothers
resigned their posts. Edesius went back to Tyre; but
Frumentius went to Alexandria, where he implored the
holy Archbishop, St. Athanasius, to send some missionaries to plant the faith in Ethiopia, and to appoint a
Bishop for that vast empire.   St. Athanasius called a
Synod of Bishops, and, by their advice, resolved to
ordain St. Frumentius himself as chief pastor, judg-
ing no one more fit to finish the work he had begun.
Frumentius, invested with this episcopal character,
went back to Axuma, and the conversion of the whole
nation followed. The young king and his brother

received baptism, and added all the weight of their example and authority to the apostolic labours of the holy Bishop. The Arian Emperor Constantine summoned the two kings to deliver up Frumentius into the hands of George, the barbarous invader of the see of St. Athanasius. But the Ethiopians paid no regard to the emperor's menaces; so the saint continued to feed and defend his flock till it pleased the Chief Shepherd to call him home. In the Apology of St. Athanasius, Constantine's letter to the king is inserted. But this threatened storm served only to increase the love and zeal of the new converts; and very soon the cross was lifted up from Mecca to Melinda, and from Syene to the Equator. When in Egypt the true faith began to be threatened by Arianism on the one hand, and by the Nestorian and Eutychian heresies on the other, Abyssinia became the refuge of the persecuted Catholics, and her mountains and deserts were soon peopled with monasteries following the Rule of the Solitaries of Egypt.* It was soon after this that the whole of Arabia was conquered by Caleb, better known under the title of Elesbaan, the Constantine or Charlemagne of Ethiopia,—a man of wonder-

---

* Tradition, and various ancient chronicles, have preserved the names of nine of these monasteries, which were called, from their holy founders: Abba Za Michael, Abba Garima, Abba Licanos, Abba Pantaleone, Abba Abzé, Abba Gubba, Abba Imeata, Abba Aleph, and Abba Frama. They adhered to the Council of Chalcedon, and used the Latin chants and rite.

ful courage and character, and of earnest and devoted
piety. A Jew named Zonovas, or Dunaan, had become King of Arabia, and, inflamed with the greatest
hatred against the Catholic faith, had massacred and
tortured Christians of every age and class, including
420 priests and religious, both nuns and monks, whom
he burnt at the stake, after having given them the
choice of apostasy or death. The Catholic emperor
at Constantinople, informed of these proceedings, wrote
to the Patriarch of Alexandria, to implore him to induce the good King Elesbaan to avenge the Christians
in Arabia, and save the remnant which the tyrant
had left. The Patriarch sent him, together with the
emperor's missive, a consecrated Host, with an earnest
entreaty that he would undertake this holy war. Elesbaan instantly assembled his troops, and marched to
the assistance of the persecuted Christians. The Jewish
King Dunaan was defeated in a pitched battle, and
killed by Elesbaan's own hand. Elesbaan reëstablished the Christian religion throughout the land, and
replaced the Bishop, Gregentius, in his see; building,
likewise, over the site of the martyrdom of those holy
confessors, a beautiful church to contain their relics.
Having accomplished his purposes, this good king
returned to Ethiopia, where, soon after, he resigned
the throne in favour of his son; and, sending his
crown to be laid on the Sepulchre at Jerusalem, he
retired into a cave in the desert, where, abandoning

all earthly grandeur, he spent the rest of his life in practices of the most austere penance and devotion.*

His son, Ghebra Mascal, following in his father's steps, became equally beloved by the people, and by his courage and valour maintained the ascendency of Ethiopia over all the surrounding countries. This state of things lasted for some centuries ; when a circumstance arose which changed the whole position of affairs, and for the first time introduced into the country those seeds of error and heresy, which have since borne such terrible fruits. The Catholic Archbishop of Abyssinia having died, ambassadors were sent as usual to demand a successor of the Patriarch of Alexandria. To their surprise, they found the see vacant, and the patriarchal chair filled by a usurper named Abba Benjamin, who had intrigued with the Arabs to banish the Catholic Archbishop and those of his communion, and to establish the Copts in their stead. The Arabs, however, would not let Benjamin reign in Alexandria, so that he set up his episcopal see at Cairo. The Abyssinians, unwilling to return empty-handed to their own country, accepted the Bishop pressed upon them by Benjamin, together with certain monks as his coadjutors. But no sooner were

* M. Sapeto discovered at Axuma, and in the mountains near, various descriptions of the reign of this Elesbaan, whom they denominated the "Holy King." At this time, also, the Arabic language passed into Ethiopia, which language henceforth became a mixture of the two dialects.

these men arrived in Abyssinia, than they began to
propagate their Eutychian heresy, and a civil war was
declared. The Catholics refused to have any thing to
say to these new doctrines; and a great number took
refuge in the neighbouring states, and founded religious houses beyond the jurisdiction of the Coptic
Bishop. A violent religious persecution arose—ending
in a subversion of almost all religion; and the grossest
abuses and superstitions became gradually mingled
with the faith of the people, which remain to this
day, and have almost destroyed all traces of Christianity. The monastic state remains; but so degenerated, that it scarcely deserves the name. In 1452
the reigning king, disgusted with the enormous taxes
levied by the heretical Patriarch on his people, resolved
to petition Rome for a successor to the episcopal
chair then vacant. But his two ambassadors were
murdered at Alexandria, by order of the Sultan, having
been betrayed by a slave. In 1520 the Portuguese
sent an embassy to this almost unknown land, and a
few years later, at the entreaty of the Abyssinians,
returned in greater numbers and rescued them from
the dominion of the Turks, who had overrun the country
and tried to establish the Mahometan faith.

St. Ignatius of Loyola, hearing of the melancholy
religious state of the people, implored the Pope's permission to go there; but being refused, he sent two
of his disciples, Oviedo and Lopez; who penetrated

into the interior of the country, and by their heroic
charity and patience converted thousands to the true
faith. Both died, however, in 1597; and then little
was done till, in 1603, another of their congregation, Father Paez, undertook this difficult mission.
Few of the Company of Jesus have surpassed this holy
priest in Apostolic zeal, courage, and wisdom. Avoid-
ing controversy, and keeping clear from all political
parties or court intrigues, he laboured steadily in
his holy vocation, winning multitudes of souls to Christ
by no other arms than those of silence, charity, and
prayer. The king, charmed with his conversation
and manners, became himself a convert, and sent to
Rome a written profession of his faith. The greater
portion of the court and the aristocracy followed the
example of their sovereign, and declared themselves
Catholics. Father Paez was a wonderfully learned
man, versed in every human science; a great mathe-
matician, mechanic, linguist, and historian. He had
also a wonderful knowledge of medicine and of various
manual arts, and taught the Abyssinians how to carve
both in wood and stone; so that by the versatility of his
genius he won over people of every sort to that which
was the one aim of his life—their conversion to God.
He died in 1624, amidst the tears of the whole population, in whose memory he ever lives as a saint—and
with him perished the mission; which day by day
declined, till the remaining Jesuits were banished or

martyred by the apostate Emperor Fasilidas. In
1648, the Propaganda sent four Capuchins to replace
them; but they only got as far as Suakin, when they
were beheaded by the inhabitants. In the time of
Louis XIV. a Franciscan monk was sent, together
with a doctor; but both died before they arrived at
their destination. Again, in 1751, the Franciscans
attempted to revive the mission, but met with the
same fate as their predecessors. At last, in 1838,
a M. Sapeto, with two other French gentlemen, arrived at Adoua, the capital of Tigré. Abyssinia had
ceased to be under the dominion of one emperor, but
was divided into a multitude of petty states with
independent sovereigns. The King of Tigré, Oubié,
received the Europeans with great cordiality; and a
little Catholic congregation by degrees gathered round
them, composed of about a hundred persons, who sent
in a formal profession of faith to Pope Gregory XVI.,
with a request for a priest to be sent to instruct them.
This was the origin of the mission undertaken by the
Lazarist Fathers; and the leader of this expedition,
which might almost have been called a "forlorn hope,"
is the man whose history we now propose to give to
our readers.

Justin de Jacobis was born at Sta. Fele, in the
Basilicate, which is a province of the Neapolitan
kingdom, on the 10th October 1800. He was the
seventh out of fourteen children, and was indebted to

his holy mother for his first impressions of religion and virtue. She trained him early to habits of devotion, self-denial, and charity; of which she herself set him the brightest example. She accustomed him, while very young, to setting apart fixed times for meditation and mental prayer, and used to give him little presents of money and other things when he had persevered in these exercises longer than usual. His nature was quick and impatient of control, and he had a passion for every species of amusement; but he learned so well to subdue himself, that among his brothers and sisters he was called " Old Sober-sides." During his boyhood, his family removed to Naples; and there his mother chose a very holy Carmelite Father, from Monte Sancto, as his confessor, who strengthened the good dispositions his mother had instilled, and led him to live more and more above earthly things. Full of tenderness and kindness for his brothers, he bore their little teasing and their different tempers with wonderful patience; and whenever he had an opportunity, he practised a variety of small bodily mortifications,—such as going without his luncheon, or the like, and distributing any good thing that was given to him among the poor. At the same time, he was very merry and cheerful, and shared in the games of the rest with as much zest as he did in their studies, in which he soon made extraordinary progress. Monsignor Spaccapietra, now Archbishop

of Smyrna, writing of his boyhood, says : " We were
at the same college, and attended the same classes; and,
somehow or other, he was never at fault. The great
characteristic of his life was *earnestness*, and he carried
it into whatever he undertook. On the 17th October
1818, we entered together into the congregation of
the Lazarist Mission ; and so I passed not only the
time at the seminary with him, but also through all
the higher studies of philosophy and theology. The
thing which struck me most was his extraordinary
regularity and exactitude in every thing. His
humility was quite wonderful : instead of being disposed to ' show off,' as most young men are, he
always hid his talents as much as possible; and if in
reading at table, or on any other occasion, he made a
mistake in pronunciation, or was found fault with, he
was sure to bring up the subject at the hour of recreation, so as to make others laugh at what he called his
' incapacity.' His piety was more hidden, but just
as remarkable ; whenever he was ' missing,' he was
sure to be in the chapel. His devotion to the Blessed
Virgin was such, that he used to spend the time of
recreation in relating every story he could pick up
which tended to increase a love for her, and made a
sort of little exercise of it,—which the master of the
novices forbade at last, thinking that such incessant
application was hurtful to him after his meals. At
table he was noted for his wonderful abstinence, and

for always choosing what was least nice or tempting.
Except soup, which he generally took and finished,
he rarely touched any thing else. He practised continual corporal penances, and got permission to take
the discipline every day. In his studies, though
decidedly above the average, he used always to fancy
himself stupid and incapable. He often said to me
that 'he was so afraid of not being allowed to make
his vows, from his want of ability and talent.' I used
to try and reassure him, but seldom succeeded in
shaking his convictions of his own incapacity : 'Any
how, I shall never be any thing but a most miserable
little missionary,' he exclaimed one day, when we
had been discussing our future lives. On different
occasions, when he might have distinguished himself,
he always drew back and put others forward, to the
despair of his masters, who knew of how much he was
capable. He was a wonderful linguist; which he
afterwards proved by the facility with which he learned
the difficult dialects of Ethiopia, and the admirable
manner in which he both preached and wrote in those
barbarous languages. When the time came for his
ordination, his humility made him shrink from it to
such an extent that his directors almost despaired of
persuading him to become a priest : he only implored
to be employed as a coadjutor or lay brother. Another of his characteristics deserves mention ; and that
was the extraordinary way in which he gave him-

self up, as it were, to his companions, never seeming
to have a wish, or a taste, or a will of his own,—
ready to walk, or talk, or sit down, or get up, or any
thing the others wished,—so much so, that we nick-
named him (like another eminent missionary, M. Re-
zasco) '*Do what you will.*' Appointed as infirmarian
to the students, it would be difficult to describe with
what tenderness and love he discharged his duties. He
spent every moment that he could spare by the bed-
sides of his patients, consoling and comforting them
by all the means in his power. At the same time,
he did not like any one to have too strong or exclusive an affection for himself. I recollect his saying to
me one day : ' My dear brother, you show me more
love and attention than I like' (it was quite true,
for I loved him more than all the rest) : ' we never
shall make good missionaries, if we allow ourselves to
be led away by natural feelings of that sort.' Being
a great lover of poverty, he chose for himself whatever others threw away. Nothing vexed him more
than to be given a new cassock or habit ; he always
found a good reason for passing it on to another, so
as to appropriate the shabbiest and least respectable
clothes in the house. Although I have said so much,
I feel I cannot relate many anecdotes of this saint of
God during these his first years in the Congregation of St. Vincent, because his life was so hidden as
to be almost unknown to us. The keynote of it was,

Amo nesciri et pro nihilo reputari. He hid himself
as much as he could from other people's observation ;
indeed, he hid himself *from himself*, for he could see
nothing in his own conduct but misery and imperfection.
In spite of that, however, it was impossible to be in
the house with him without finding out his wonderful
and rare qualities ; while his gentleness, loving-kind-
ness, and courtesy endeared him to every one about
him. He was particularly agreeable in conversation ;
and full of fun and wit and *bons mots*, when, from any
motives of kindness or of charity, he wanted to amuse
or cheer any one, or to win them to the love of God.

" He had the greatest respect for age, and used to
beg to be allowed to wait on the old missionaries,
rendering them every kind of little loving office, and
listening to their words with the most marked attention, saying, ' they were more filled with the original
spirit of our holy founder than younger men.' He
always chose one of these as his confessor, and they
used to say of him, *dilectus Deo et hominibus.* These
words, in fact, were a *résumé* of his whole life."

His studies being ended, and being fairly embarked
in the missionary work which he had embraced, he was
sent by his superiors to a house in the diocese of Naples,
called Oria. Here he devoted himself entirely to the
care of the poor peasants, which had always been his
great ambition. One of his companions in this mission, M. Modeste Jandoli, writes of him as follows:

C

"Soon after his ordination as priest, M. de Jacobis was sent to us. He had not been in the house a week before we were all struck by his wonderful holiness and self-abnegation. He worked indefatig- ably, and was never idle for one moment. He seemed also to be so dead to himself as not to have a wish or a desire. When it was his turn to preach, the effect of his words was perfectly marvellous. Very soon the church became too small to hold the crowds who flocked to hear him. His confessional was besieged by people of every age and rank; he was at the disposal of every one, never dreaming of rest or recreation; so that he was often kept in the church till a very late hour at night. But the four-o'clock bell, the following morning, found him always in his place with the rest. Thus he passed the time till the end of the year 1829. His superiors then sent him to assist M. Jovinelli in founding a new mission at Monopoli. There was a good deal of district-visiting to be done there, and M. de Jacobis had the most wonderful success, not only by the dying beds of his penitents, but also in reconciling enemies and healing long-standing feuds in families. As the mission was in its infancy, every thing was very miserable and uncomfortable, and M. de Jacobis lived himself in a wretched little room, without air, and with scarcely any furniture. They had only two lay brothers besides themselves, and their food was the broken victuals which they could obtain here and there. M. Jovinelli broke down completely under the hardships of his position, and returned home to his family, where he soon after died. M. de Jacobis persevered until the year 1834, when he was appointed superior of the house of Lecca. During the latter part of his stay at Monopoli, a fresh religious order wished to establish themselves in the place, and, in order to do so, subjected our holy missionary to every sort of petty annoyance and persecution, and even public humiliation, the whole of which he bore with unequalled patience and forbearance. An event happened just before his departure which still further strengthened the belief of the people in his extraordinary virtues and sanctity. A M. Michel Pepe, being at the point of death, wished to make his confession, and receive the last Sacraments from M. de Jacobis. He sent an express to Monopoli, and the messenger arrived just as M. de Jacobis was going up into the pulpit to preach. The sermon over, M. de Jacobis instantly started off to accompany him, though it was in the depth of winter, and pitch-dark; the wind blew out their lantern, and they would have infallibly lost their way, had not a marvellous light surrounded M. de Jacobis—just as it happened on a similar occasion to St. Andrew Avellino—and followed him to the house of the dying man. Arrived at his destination, M. de Jacobis went at once into the sick-room, and Mme. Pepe prepared some supper for the messenger who had accompanied him. To her surprise, he would not eat; and, on being pressed to tell the reason, he mentioned what had happened, and said it had made such an impression upon him as to deprive him of all wish for either food or sleep. M. de Jacobis, being himself questioned as to the occurrence, answered, with a smile, that he supposed it was some meteor. But this was only the veil which his humility tried to throw over the whole matter, to which he never would allow the smallest allusion."

In his new position as superior, M. de Jacobis showed, if possible, even greater humility and self-abnegation than before. He made himself, in fact, the servant of all. By prudence and economy, he soon collected enough money to restore the church at Lecca, which had been much neglected; but he refused any personal advantage for any member of his own family, declining in any way to make use of his influence on their behalf. Day and night he laboured for Christ's poor. If he ever said a word which had wounded one of his community, he would ask pardon for it publicly, so as to increase his own humiliation. Already the thirst for foreign missionary work was upon him; he established a society for collecting alms for this purpose, and had little circulars printed for distribution throughout the country.

Mgr. Spaccapietra, again, writing about him at

this time, says, "After our college life was over, we were necessarily separated for some years; but all I heard confirmed my early impressions of his sanctity. M. Sparano, his superior at Oria, said, 'It was impossible to find a more perfect missionary.' His way of preaching delighted every one, and yet there was nothing very remarkable in his style. It was the *whole heart* that he put into his words which produced such an effect. Sometimes he was accused of giving absolution too easily; but he had learned from our Lord's example how to convert and lead souls by ways of love and tenderness, and the results proved that he knew human nature better than his accusers. When I went to see him in his Lecca mission (having accompanied M. Fiorillo, who was apostolic visitor), I was witness to the way in which he was positively adored by his whole community. As we were going over the house, and passing through the kitchen, the brother who was acting as cook came up to complain to him that his colleague would not go into the garden to gather some tomatoes. 'Oh, very well,' replied he, 'give me the basket.' The brother obeyed, thinking, of course, that he was going to insist on the duty being fulfilled. But, without saying a word, M. de Jacobis went out, gathered what was necessary, and brought the vegetable to the cook, saying quietly, 'Here are your tomatoes,' to the inexpressible confusion of both the lay brothers, who fell on their knees

to ask his pardon. He only smiled, and left them.
It used to be his habit to wake the rest in the morning,
as he was always first up, and had generally spent
some little time in the tribune of the chapel before
any one else was stirring. He was only superior of
this house for a short time; having, soon after his
election, been chosen by Rome for the Abyssinian
mission. During this period, his good mother died,
to the inexpressible grief of her son, who, however,
would himself sing her Requiem Mass, and afterwards
accompany the body to the cemetery. But, in spite of
his efforts, nature would make itself felt; and before the
ceremony was over, M. de Jacobis fainted dead away in
the arms of one of the brothers who had accompanied
him. . . I was asked, soon after this, to help him in giving
a retreat at the convent of St. Nicolas de Tolentino at
Naples. Although he was older than I, and had more
years of vocation, he insisted on making me preach,
and confining himself to the catechising and confessions between. This was a device of his humility, as
he knew very well that his sermons would have brought
him great credit and honour. Afterwards he stayed
some time in the house as director of the novices.
In this work his zeal knew no bounds—nothing would
content him short of perfection; but the novices had
the tenderest veneration for their director, and
obeyed his lightest word. About this time, the cholera
broke out at Naples with great violence. He devoted

himself at once to the care of the sick, very often going out at daybreak and not returning till the middle of the night, without having taken even a crumb of bread. Endless conversions to God were the result of his labours. Men who had refused the last Sacraments and yielded to despair were won over by his loving persuasions, and died in peace with God and man. When the news came of his appointment by Cardinal Tranzoni to the Abyssinian mission, he was quite overjoyed. The only thing that troubled him was the fact of the order having come directly from the Sacred College of the Propaganda, as he feared it might not have emanated from his immediate superiors of the Congregation of the Mission. He could not rest till he had made a journey to Paris to renew his vows of submission and obedience to the Father-General, and to have his mission ratified and confirmed by him. This he easily obtained, and then came back to Naples, overflowing with happiness, to make the necessary preparations for his departure."

When this became known, the despair of the people knew no bounds. One lady wrote to remonstrate with Mgr. Spaccapietra because he had not used his influence to prevent his departure. The answer of this holy priest was as follows:

" Madam,—May God forgive you for having by your letter thrown salt and vinegar into an ever-open wound. Do you think, if I could have retained my

oldest and dearest friend, that I should have remained with my hands crossed in the matter? No;
I fear neither my faith nor my courage would have
been equal to such a sacrifice. But it is God who
will have him for this terrible Abyssinian mission, so
that, following in the steps of the great Apostles of
old, he may leave us far behind in the glorious race.
Neither M. Fiorillo, nor even our Father-General,
had any thing to do with this appointment. It was
the Cardinal Prefect of the Propaganda who, knowing his extraordinary merits, selected him for the
work. Hardly was this done, when three Abyssinian
deputies arrived in Rome to implore the Holy Father
to send some one to instruct them in the faith, and
to claim also the protection of France. M. de Jacobis
was at once commissioned to accompany them to
Paris. So all has been overruled by the Providence
of God, who is determined he shall be both saint and
martyr. But that does not prevent my being broken-
hearted, like yourself, at losing him. However, it is
God's doing: may His holy and adorable will be
done! This is my only answer."

The local papers echoed the regrets and sorrow
felt by the whole town at this irreparable loss. After
dwelling on the virtues we have before enumerated,
the leading journal of the day goes on to say: " Miracles have not been wanting to attest the wonderful
graces which the Most High has showered on his

labours. We have seen the barren woman become the joyful mother of children ; the dead restored to life; abundant harvests and fisheries given ; the insane restored to their right mind ;—and all from the effect of his prayers. And it is a man like this whom we are about to lose!—unless the Holy Father will put a curb on his desire for martyrdom, and compel him to remain amongst us. Already are his preparations made for this Ethiopian mission; and what awaits him there? Persecution from within and from without: pagans, Mussulmans, and heretics, all combined against him with bitter hatred and invincible obstinacy; which, without the burning sun of that unhealthy land, acting on a frame already weakened by austerities and devotion to others, will speedily bring about the end for which he has been so long thirsting. If the Sovereign Pontiff will deign to listen to our prayer, we would implore him to leave us a man indispensable to the cause of religion in his own land, and who, more than 'the righteous' of Holy Writ, will save our Sodom, and avert God's anger from His people. Whatever may be the decision of the Holy Father, we have at least acquitted our own consciences, by making known to him the great gifts which God has lavished on this His servant; and by telling him something of the noble nature of one whom Europe is on the point of losing for ever."

CHAPTER II.

Mgr. de Jacobis starts on his Abyssinian mission—His difficulties on his first arrival—His visit to Rome.

M. DE JACOBIS, deaf to the voice of nature or the entreaties of his friends, started for his mission in the summer of 1839, accompanied by one of his fellow-missionaries, a Lazarist and a Neapolitan like himself, M. Louis Montuori. The steamer which conveyed them to Alexandria had two other Lazarist mission-aries on board, bound for Syria,. MM. Poussou and Reygasse. The voyage was short; but even during that time an event occurred which is attested by M. Reygasse, who is now superior of the mission at Tripoli. "When we arrived at Malta," he writes, "and after we had each said our Mass in the church of St. John, M. Poussou and I wanted to go and see the tombs of the Knights Templars, and left M. de Jacobis to say his Mass in the same church. When we came back, we were very much astonished to see a whole crowd of people come running up to us, who had just been assisting at M. de Jacobis' Mass, and who exclaimed one after the other: 'Gentlemen, who is this saint you have brought with you? We distinctly saw the Infant Jesus above his head, from the

moment of the Elevation till after the Communion.'
Of this we never dared say a word to him."

The two missionaries reached Abyssinia in September 1839. They had been preceded by M. Sapeto,
a Piedmontese, and one of the same congregation;
and were well received by the King of Tigré, Oubié,
who soon discovered what a treasure he had acquired
in M. de Jacobis. Our holy missionary laid down as a
rule for his future conduct, never to meddle in politics;
to be on good terms with the king and his court,
but to keep aloof from both; to avoid any irritating
controversies, and to preach by acts more than by
words; to cultivate the affection of the Coptic priests
and *Defteras*, or doctors; and to avoid any religious
foundation, which at the beginning might have given
rise to fear or jealousy. He himself remained at
first in the Tigré province, and the two other missionaries went on to that of Amara, the scene of Father
Paez's labours. Here the hatred against the Jesuits
still existed, and every year the people came to take
the dust from their sepulchres and throw it to the
winds. But MM. Sapeto and Montuori were well
received by the king, Ras-Aly, and by the superior of
the Coptic monastery.

At the end of five years there were already a good
many Catholics in the province; but M. Sapeto's
health compelled him to give it up and return to
Cairo, and M. Montuori remained alone at Gondar.

During this time, what became of M. de Jacobis?
Settled at Adoua, the capital of the province of Tigré,
and knowing the way in which Europeans were despised
by the natives, he took a new method of overcoming
their prejudices, and that was by intense humility.
Every day he went to the Abyssinian church to pray
and recite his Breviary.   But he could not say Mass
there, nor could he do so in a private house, which
would have given scandal.   The first months, therefore, were passed in patient silence.   It was necessary
to make acquaintance with the people, and to conci-
liate their chiefs.   But patience and silence did not
imply idleness.   Three languages are current in the
country : the *Gheez,* or sacred tongue ; the *Tigré;*
and the *Amaric.*   M. de Jacobis devoted all his ener-
gies to mastering these difficult and apparently hopeless languages; and succeeded so marvellously that,
on the 26th January 1840 (only four months after
his arrival in the country), he could hold a conference in the *Amaric* tongue with a certain number of
people who had taken pity on his isolation and came
to visit him.   He found them extremely ignorant,
and the most learned among them asserted that there
were three Gods.   However, the good seed was
sown, and began to germinate.   Many were ready
and eager to be taught, and willing to renounce their
errors.   It was a great step gained, to change their
ideas as to what was meant by the Catholic faith.

Then M. de Jacobis thought the time was come when he could speak more openly to the people. He called a conference of all the priests of Adoua, and addressed them in their own tongue, and with an eloquence which touched every heart. We will give a short *résumé* of his speech, which was in the Oriental style, and as follows :

"The mouth speaks the language of the heart, of which the tongue is the key. When I open my mouth, I unlock the door of my heart. Come and see how the Holy Spirit of God has filled my soul with tender love for my Christian brothers in Ethiopia. I was in my own land ; there I heard about you. I said to my father and to my mother, 'Give me your blessing, and I will go.' 'Whither?' they exclaimed. 'I want to go to my dear brothers in Abyssinia, and tell them how I love them. Yes, I leave you, O my father! I leave you, O my mother! I love you very much, but I love my brothers in Abyssinia more.' Then did they answer me : 'But we shall never see you again! The way is long—you must traverse the sea and the desert—there are tempests and serpents and lions in your path.' And I replied: 'No, we shall never meet again;' and my father shed tears, and my mother wept ; but they gave me their blessing, and said : 'Go, my son, where God calls you. Go and see your Abyssinian brothers, and tell them that we also love them, for we have sent them the son who is so dear to us.' And then I knelt and cried, and received their blessing. O my friends, what bitter tears we shed—they and I ! My eyes are still dimmed with the thought. But the love I felt for you was so strong—stronger than the parting— stronger than death itself! I shut my eyes, that I might not see their tears—I shut my ears, that I might not hear their groans—and I went forth. In the midst of storms and tempests, one cry only was in my heart: 'Lord, let me see my brothers in Abyssinia before I die!' In the desert, amidst the wild beasts, one prayer only was on my lips: 'Lord, let me hear the Abyssinian voice; and then, if Thou wilt, I am ready to die.' God heard my petition —He preserved me from all evil. Now I am here, and have seen you, and I am content. Let Him grant me life, be it short or long; as many days as He gives me, I consecrate them to you: for it is for you alone that He has given them to me. My life is in your hands. If you wish for my blood, come, open my veins, and take it to the last drop; it is all yours! To die by your hands would be joy to me. But if you wish me to live, every hour of my life shall be spent for you. For you I will pray, I will study, I will toil. If you are sorrowful, I will come and comfort you in our dear Lord's name; if you are poor, I will help you for His sake; if you are naked, I will cover you with my own garments; if you are hungry, you shall have my last bit of bread; if you are sick, I will come and nurse you, and watch by your bedside; if you wish me to teach you, I will impart to you all I know. I have nothing left on earth—neither father, nor mother, nor home, nor country. There only remain to me God and my brothers in Abyssinia. Look into my heart and see! Only *He* is there, and you. For whom does my poor heart burn? For my Lord and His Abyssinian children. Therefore, I will do what you will. If you wish me to stay with you, I will stay; to go away from you, I will go; to speak in your churches, I will speak; to keep silence, I will be mute. I am a priest, preacher, and confessor like you. Do you wish me to say Mass? I will say it;— to hear confessions? I will do so;—to preach? I will do that likewise. Do you wish me to leave it all alone? I will then do nothing. Now I have opened my heart to you, and placed the key in your hands. If you ask me who I am, I can only answer: ' I am a Christian from Rome, who loves the Abyssinians.' If any one inquires : ' Who is this stranger ?' you must answer: ' He is a European Christian, who loves the Ethiopian Christians better than friends, or relations, or father, or mother; for he has left them all to come and tell them how he loves them.' I have now been for four months in your country. You have seen and known and conversed with me. Tell me if I have caused any scandal, or done you any harm? I do not think so. But if I have as yet done you no wrong, I have not until now been able to do you any good. Now, I wish to change my conduct in this respect. I want to be not only your friend, but your slave. I wish to spend myself, and be spent, for you and yours. O my Lord and Saviour, in whose presence I am, Thou knowest that I lie not!"

This speech produced a wonderful effect on the people; and his voice and manner would, indeed, have touched a heart of stone. Already they had been surprised at seeing this stranger spend days and nights in the church, absorbed in prayer; the priests and monks ceased to mistrust him, and began to feel that there was something saint-like and extraordinary about him. They invited him to hold a public conference, and to discuss the points of difference between the Catholic and Coptic priesthood; and his speech on this occasion has been preserved in his Journal, from which we will give a short summary:

"After forty centuries of desire and sighs and tears on the part of the Patriarchs and Prophets, appeared the Messiah. What did He not do and suffer to bring men out of darkness into His marvellous light? He founded His Church in His precious Blood. To this Church He gave a head, to be His Vicar upon earth; and that head, as the Gospel tells you, was St. Peter. After preaching in Antioch, and

Pontus, and Cappadocia, and Bithynia, St. Peter
established his see in Rome. St. Mark accompanied
him there, and was sent by him to Alexandria. He
died in the year 63; and then a successor was appointed from Rome to fill the vacant see of Alexandria.
On this point we are all agreed; and in this belief
the first Patriarchs of Alexandria lived and died for
450 years after the death of Christ. A holy friendship, a close and intimate relationship, existed, then,
between the successors of St. Mark and the successors
of the see of Peter. They were united by the most
sacred ties. Listen to the voice of one of these Patriarchs : ' Whosoever does not acknowledge the Head
of the Church, does not belong to the Church ; whosoever is not united to the see of Peter, he is as a
withered branch of a tree which men cast into the
fire, and it is burned.' And so they spoke and wrote
and taught for centuries. But then there came a
time of sorrow and division ; like the sons of Jacob,
one was hated by the rest, and sold and delivered up
to strangers. Yet that one became powerful and
mighty, while the rest were dying of hunger. And
you, my brethren, how has it fared with you ?
Where are your Patriarchs ? where are your saints ?
While Rome—Ah ! I would I could take you there
with me. You would feel as your ancestress, the
Queen of Sheba, did, on beholding the glory of
Solomon. Why have you been separated from the

D

parent tree? Recollect what happened when Jacob's
children met again after their long and cruel separa-
tion. They fell on one another's neck with tears,
and made peace—a lasting peace. Ah! if we would
but do the same, and have one faith, one hope, one
baptism! One faith! the faith of Jesus Christ, as
preserved to us by His Vicar on earth. One love!
the love of our Lord, as taught us in His Gospel. It
is this faith and this love which I am come to preach,
and that not for the sake of sordid gain or of gold. I
seek for nothing; I fear nothing. Throw me into
your vilest dungeon, deliver me up into the hands of
your most cruel executioner, and then ask me, ' What
I came to this country for?' I shall answer, ' For the
love of you, my Abyssinian brothers, and to save your
souls.' If my words please you, what prevents our
being *one?* I am a Roman Catholic; be the same, as
your forefathers were; and let us labour together for
this people, plunged in superstition and vice, and in
worse than pagan errors. If my plan displeases you,
send for the executioner. I am ready and glad to die for
the faith of my Lord and Master. The voice of my blood
will mount to Heaven; but it will not call for vengeance
on you, as did the blood of Abel; but for mercy, like
the Blood of Jesus, for whose love I would joyfully
give my life. And then our dear Lord will send you
another preacher, not laden with sins and infirmities
like myself, but holy and blameless and pure in His

sight: and he will say to you the same words as mine, for truth is *one*. You will listen to his voice, and you will become one fold under one Shepherd, Jesus Christ our Lord."

This conference caused a great sensation. Many of the *Defteras*, or doctors, exclaimed, " This priest speaks the words of truth and reason; let him be our father!" Many conversions followed. But the greatest obstacle arose from the corruption of morals, which in Abyssinia is almost universal. Purity, self-denial, self-abnegation, are the watchwords of Catholicism : and he whose heart is not opened to accept these principles is little disposed to embrace the true faith. A whole host of prejudices had likewise been engendered in the minds of the people against the Catholic Church, for heresy is the same in every age and country. At last our holy missionary felt that the most important step would be to induce some of the most influential of the inhabitants to accompany him to Europe, so as to let them judge for themselves and see with their own eyes the absurdity of the allegations which they had heard all their lives against the Church of God. His wish was brought about sooner than he anticipated. On the 2d January 1841, the prince of the country, Oubié, sent for him, and received him with the greatest honours. The following week was fixed upon for a more important audience ; and for this, M. de Jacobis prepared himself

by earnest prayer and by the holy Sacrifice. "Put into
my mouth, O Lord, the words which I shall speak, so
that they may touch the heart of this infidel king!"
Such was his burning petition ; and it was granted.
Oubié received him even more graciously than before,
accepting his presents according to Oriental custom,
and making him sit on his own carpet in the midst
of his court. After the usual compliments, Oubié
told him that he wished him to accompany a deputation into Egypt to demand a new Bishop (Abouna) of
the Coptic Patriarch ; he added, that it was more a
political than a religious mission, and that Monsignor.
de Jacobis could accompany the deputies without in
any way compromising his faith. M. de Jacobis at
first consented ; but, after a little reflection, he became
alarmed lest this step should be construed by Catholics into a connivance with error. He returned,
therefore, to the king, and exclaimed :

"Most mighty prince ! I am a Catholic, and
as such I will live and die. I might indeed
accompany your deputation into Egypt, preserving
in my heart my sacred faith ; but what scandal
might I not give to my co-religionists ! what sorrow to my father and master, the Pontiff of Rome !
On such terms I cannot—I will not—go." These
words, spoken with all the anguish of conviction, did
not, as he expected, rouse the anger of the king.
He therefore, after a pause, continued with greater

boldness : " On one condition only will I accompany
your deputies ; and that is, that I may strive to
bring about a reunion between the Coptic Patriarch
and the see of Rome, from which he is now so un-
happily divided. I will go, if thereby the obstacles
may be removed which at present prevent my building Catholic churches in your kingdom. I will go,
if your deputies will accompany me afterwards to
Rome ; if not to tender their submission to the successor of St. Peter, at least to implore his friendship
and protection as that of the most powerful of earthly
sovereigns." And so saying, he unrolled a map to
show the king and his courtiers how vast was the
extent of the Holy Pontiff's power, as compared with
the kingdom of Abyssinia.

One might have imagined, after so audacious a
speech, that there would be an end of the Abyssinian
mission, and that its bold missionary would instantly
be put to death by the indignant despot. But the
hearts of kings are in the hands of God, who moulds
them to His will.

From that moment the mission started into life,
after having appeared almost hopeless. The king,
instead of being angry, replied with calmness and affability that all the conditions asked would be granted :
that M. de Jacobis should go to Cairo, to have a
conference with the Patriarch, and strive to incline
him to unity ; that he should be the bearer of a letter

from himself to the Patriarch in this sense, asking,
likewise, for permission to erect Catholic churches in
the country; and that he might take the deputation on
to Rome, by whom he would send an autograph
letter to the Holy See expressive of his respect and
veneration. As a proof of the sincerity of his pro-
fessions, Oubié accepted with great joy a portrait of
the Holy Father which M. de Jacobis had received from
the Propaganda, together with a medal struck on the
occasion of the last canonisation. He had before
accepted a picture of the Blessed Virgin, representing
her miraculous apparition.

Nothing, therefore, appeared to threaten the success of the expedition ; the journey was decided upon,
and it was arranged that it should be begun in a few
days. Of course, in all this matter, Oubié's own views
were purely political. Believing in the *prestige* of
France, and that its support would strengthen his
throne, he omitted no means of ingratiating himself with
her missionaries, and thereby winning her good opinion ;
but God overrules all earthly things for His great ends.

On the 21st January 1841, M. de Jacobis started
for Massouah. The chief of the deputation was a
relation of the king's, L'Allaca Apta-Salassia, Director of Public Instruction, and Prime Minister :
the rest were taken from the most eminent of the
priesthood and the monastic orders ; together with
Abba Ghebra Mikael, a very learned man, and the

first physician in the kingdom. The day of their departure was one of real triumph for our holy missionary—men and women of every rank and age followed his mule weeping, and praying that his good angel might accompany him, and bring him back to them in safety. Some of the children could only be restrained from following him by being tied hand and foot by their parents; his scholars all loved him like a father—one of them, with tears and sobs, besought him to take him with him : " I want to go to Rome with you, and to learn ; my mother will not let me ; —may I not come without her knowledge?" M. de Jacobis in reply told him to repeat the Ten Commandments to him in Amaric, which he did. When the boy had arrived at the fourth—"Thou shalt honour and obey thy father and mother"—he stopped him : " Dear child, can you say those words, and yet leave your home without your mother's permission ?" The poor boy remained silent, though he continued to cry bitterly. The deputation at last started ; their progress was Oriental, and proportionally slow ; in all the countries through which they passed, they were received by the people with royal honours. But the appearance of the deputies scarcely corresponded with the magnificence of these receptions—they were badly clothed, with bare feet ; and sat on the ground, with no other bed than a bullock's skin, and with no plate but their fingers ; their meat was eaten raw, for they never lit a fire. From Massouah they embarked in little Arab boats on the Red Sea. The voyage lasted for two months. It was a most wearisome and uninteresting time for M. de Jacobis; the badly appointed boats swarmed with vermin; the crew were of the lowest sort, and brutal in manners and disposition. Often they had to lay-to for days, waiting for a favourable wind; and nothing can be more *triste* than the appearance of the Red Sea, with its barren shores and the rugged mountains beyond, especially in the brazen glare of an Eastern sun. It was not till the 4th of March that they cast anchor in the port of Djeddah. M. de Jacobis whiled away the tedium of the voyage by reflections on the marvels which had taken place on that sea on behalf of God's chosen people; and he was especially moved on Good-Friday, when preaching to the crew on the Passion of Him whom Moses had seen through a glass darkly and faintly foreshadowed—thus typifying the close connection between the Old Testament and the New.

On the 25th April they arrived at Suez; and from thence, after five days' march across the Desert, the caravan reached Cairo. Although they mustered more than fifty people, they were attacked by the Bedouins, and escaped with some difficulty out of their hands.

At Cairo, the faith of our holy missionary was put to a fresh test. The plague was devastating that capital, and all the European consulates were closed. The monks had shut themselves up in their enclosure, and allowed no intercourse with the outside world. Friends mistrusted friends; and, in the universal panic (so well described by the author of *Eothen*), every door seemed closed against our travellers. Treachery came to add to their difficulties. A Jew conducted them to the house of a nominal friend, who was in reality in league with the heretical Patriarch. All their plans were discovered and circumvented by his intrigues; and they were finally threatened with excommunication.

The monks, in terror, deserted the expedition, and started for Jerusalem. In the midst of all this, the plague broke out amongst the caravan, and seven of their number fell victims to the fell disease, among whom was a young Catholic doctor of eminent piety, who had won the hearts of the whole party.

In order to gain the deputies over to his side, the Patriarch now began to treat them with great consideration—invited them to his own house, ordained several as priests and deacons; but threatened them with the dire vengeance of Heaven if they presumed to hold intercourse with the Catholic priest. They so far yielded to his representations, as to decide to suppress the king's (Oubié's) letters, urging the reconciliation with the Holy See, and asking permission to build Catholic churches. The hour was now come for M. de

Jacobis to interfere. Taking with him Clot-Bey, the
celebrated Frenchman then in the service of the King
of Egypt, and the Chevalier Bocti, Russian consul,—
both good Arabic scholars,—he demanded, and obtained, an audience of the Patriarch, and presented
his letters and credentials from the king, of which he
fortunately had secured a duplicate. The courage and
firmness with which he spoke intimidated the Patriarch, who put on the lamb's skin, replied with smooth
and insidious words, and promised a definitive answer in
a few days. This time having elapsed, M. de Jacobis returned to the Patriarch, who received him courteously,
and offered him coffee. M. de Jacobis had been advised
to drink nothing, for fear of poison ; but, lest his not
doing so should be interpreted into an act of fear, he
simply lifted up his heart to Him who had promised
that His servants should drink deadly draughts un-
harmed, and quietly drank what was offered to him.
Several Coptic doctors were present, and the conversation began amicably ; but soon they took exception
to certain expressions in the king's letters—especially
those in which he spoke of the Pope as the " great
King of Italy," and of the " mighty protection of
France." Finally, unable to defeat M. de Jacobis in
argument, they suddenly turned round upon him with
furious abuse, declared the letters to be false, and his
own conduct grossly fraudulent ; while the Abyssinians listened in trembling silence, and never at-

tempted any defence of the holy missionary. The
Patriarch, throwing off the mask, burst into un-
governable fury, vowed that no Catholic churches
should be built either in Tigré or in any other part of
Abyssinia, and threatened with instant excommunication any of the deputies who should hold communication with M. de Jacobis, or attempt to go to Rome. He
went still further, and ordered them to return at once
to their own country, without visiting Jerusalem or the
Holy Places. This exasperated the principal deputy,
L'Allaca Apta-Salassia, who replied to the Patriarch
in bitter terms, reproaching his council, with well-
merited severity, for their hypocrisy, and then indig-
nantly left the audience-chamber. But the difficulty
was what to do, or where to go. They had placed
themselves, as it were, at the mercy of the Patriarch,
by having accepted his hospitality; and the plague
closed all other doors against them. Finally, they
decided on a middle course; which was, to follow the
monks to Jerusalem, and leave M. de Jacobis behind.

Now, this would have destroyed all the hopes of
our saint. Full well he knew why the Copts opposed
with such violence the journey to Rome : "Go *there*,"
they had said to the deputies, "and we are perfectly
sure that you will come back Roman Catholics." Already the greater portion of the deputies had been won
over by his charity and holy zeal, and had secretly ab-
jured the errors of their sect. In this strait, M. de

Jacobis, having first committed the whole affair to God, went to the Catholic Coptic Bishop, Abba-Carima, who was acting as Vicar-Apostolic, and to M. de Bourville, the excellent French consul, and with them agreed that the only possible course was to induce the Abyssinians at once to leave Cairo for Alexandria, and there decide on their future course. This proposal was, consequently, made to them; and they, desirous above all things to escape from the Patriarch's clutches, instantly acceded to the plan.

Directly after the feast of Corpus Christi, therefore, M. de Jacobis and the Abyssinian mission, amounting then to only twenty-three people, started for Alexandria. The heart of the good missionary was full of hope; and yet it was difficult to see by what means the end he had in view was to be attained. The Abyssinians trusted that, through the intervention of Mehemet Ali, they would be able to brave the Patriarch, and go to Rome. But God, as if determined to prove to them the futility of all worldly agencies, made use of a very humble instrument for the accomplishment of His designs. Neither the consuls nor the viceroy would have any thing to say to them, and the game seemed lost; when one day, as the whole party were dining with M. Rosetti, the Tuscan consul, his wife—a lady of eminent piety, and beloved by every one in Alexandria*—began

* This admirable lady died, a martyr of charity, in June 1865,

speaking of Italy and the Holy Father, and so inflamed their hearts by her descriptions, that the
deputies, springing to their feet, exclaimed to M. de
Jacobis : "Come ; let us go, and go at once. We are
unanimous." " And so," as M. de Jacobis reports in
his Journal, " the malice of our enemies was defeated
by the simple, earnest words of a holy woman—as
Mary overcame the serpent ; *digitus Dei est hic.*"

The only difficulty now remaining was a pecuniary
one. The cupidity of the Patriarch had exacted so
large a sum for the consecration of the Bishop* whom
the deputies had been instructed to ask for by the
king, that they had nothing left for the. expenses of
their voyage. This difficulty was, however, met partly
by the generosity of M. Ceruti, the Sardinian consul,
and partly by that of Cardinal Franzoni—to whom
Abyssinia owes, under God, her present mission, and
who, unexpectedly, sent M. de Jacobis a sufficient sum
for the purpose. Thus, all obstacles being removed,

having been carried off by the cholera at the same time as her
daughter, and was followed to the grave by the tears of hundreds
of poor and afflicted natives, to whom she had been as a mother.

* A letter is extant, written in the Amaric language by Deftera
Haïlo, describing the whole circumstances attending this consecration; for which they paid 4000 talaris (20,000 francs), and three valuable slaves—which latter the Patriarch presented to Mehemet Ali.
The person selected for a Bishop was a perfect boy, who strutted
about with a white pocket-handkerchief saturated with *eau de Co-
logne;* but who was unable to answer the simplest question in theology. Yet this man was appointed Bishop under the title of " Abouna
Salama," and went to Abyssinia in the month of November 1840.

the whole party embarked in the ship *Scamandre* for
Rome.   At Malta, they were detained by the quaran-
tine for several days; but M. de Jacobis' heart was too
full of thankfulness to admit of a murmuring thought.
He wrote from Malta (14th of July 1841): "This
journey will change the whole ideas of my poor Abyssinians, and render the conversion of their country
comparatively easy.   Pray for this result.   But a
little while, and the end will come, and we shall all
be united in Him to Whom the redemption of these
souls is so dear."

From Malta they touched at Naples, and, in a few
hours later, arrived at Rome, where they were received
with open arms both by the Sovereign Pontiff and by
the people, some of whom could scarcely restrain their
tears at the sight of these first-fruits of so difficult a
mission.   The Holy Father gave them a special audience, and spoke to them for a long time through the
medium of Cardinal Mezzofanti and of M. de Jacobis.
He caused King Oubié's letter to be opened, read, and
translated before him ; and accepted, with the most fa-
therly benevolence, the presents of incense, birds, and
other Abyssinian products, which they had brought to
him.   The deputies took their leave, each one only more
strongly impressed than the other with the paternal
charity and kindness with which the Holy Father had
listened to their statements, and the personal interest
he had manifested in each member of the deputation.

A few weeks later he received them again, making the chiefs sit on stools by his side, and by his tenderness and affability winning their hearts still more. He gave them medals and crosses of gold and silver, according to the rank and dignity of each; and likewise an autograph letter for their king (Oubié), full of kindness and good sense; together with some magnificent presents. One of these was a gold chain and cross, of beautiful workmanship, with an inscription, which may thus be translated : " The Blood of the Man-God is the price of our salvation."

The Abyssinians left Rome, as M. de Jacobis expected, overwhelmed with surprise and admiration. Never before having seen any thing out of their own country, the refinements of civilisation and the magnificence of every thing around them astonished them no less than the gorgeousness of the Divine worship, and the spectacle of unity and strength which Rome, above all other places on earth, presents to the Christian world. To those outside the visible unity of the Church of God, many things may appear contradictory and disordered; but seen from within, it is, like the Basilica of St. Peter's,—or like Dr. Newman's simile of a painted-glass window,—all order, harmony, and in perfect proportion. With a parting blessing from the great Head of the Church in the Piazza del Popolo, and with a vow in their hearts to live and die for him, and still more for the

faith—in defence of which one of them was eventually
to reap the crown of martyrdom—the deputies returned to Naples, where M. de Jacobis brought them
to the house of the Congregation, called *dei Vergini*;
and, whilst waiting for the vessel which was to convey them back to Africa, took them to see all that
was most interesting in that bright southern capital.
They assisted, likewise, at the great feast of the 19th
September; and, again, at one in the church of
St. Nicolas de Tolentino, in honour of the B. Virgin,
to whom the Abyssinians are specially devoted. At
vespers, M. de Jacobis preached a sermon on the propagation of the faith, and then, suddenly breaking
off, addressed the Abyssinians in their own language,
that they might understand the subject of the dis-
course—which moved them to tears, and they exclaimed, " Oh, the love and power of your holy
Catholic faith! It is we who are poor, and miserable, and blind, and naked !" This was a wonderful
admission and effect of Divine grace—for the in-
veterate pride of these people is one of the chief
obstacles to their reception of divine truth. They
imagine that out of Abyssinia nothing can be either
good or desirable—and it was mainly to correct this
impression, through the medium of men of the rank
and position of these deputies, who would be believed
on their return by their own people, that M. de Jacobis
had been so desirous of bringing about the visit to

Europe. At last, on the 5th October 1841, they reëmbarked on board the French steamer *Lycurgus*, bearing away with them the most favourable impressions of all they had seen and heard in those two remarkable cities, which, in their figurative language, they compared to the sun and the moon; and full of anxiety and zeal to impart to their own countrymen some portion, at any rate, of the light and truth which were beginning to dawn in their own hearts.

CHAPTER III.

THE first days of their voyage to Alexandria were
miserable enough, from the effects of a gale which,
at that moment, swept over the Mediterranean, and
caused many wrecks. But M. de Jacobis, who found
in every occurrence only a fresh means of sanctifying
himself and those around him, writes of these days,
" We have now, as it were, a little miniature of a
missionary's life. Calm and sunshine are not for him,
but he must pass from one tribulation to the other—
all the time with a tranquillity of mind and a peace
of soul independent of outward and untoward circumstances, which only form part of that mystery of
hidden suffering by which souls are more closely
united to our dear Lord." These words are, in fact,
a commentary on his own life, and on his favourite
text, *In omnibus tribulationem patimur, sed non an-
gustiamur.*

In an amusing letter, dated the 18th October, he
describes a "passage at arms" he had with a sturdy
British Dissenting minister, who, laying down the
axiom that *all Italy was buried in ignorance and super-*

stition, proceeded to demonstrate the fact by arguments which were neither logical nor convincing,— and which were met with a good-humoured raillery on the part of M. de Jacobis that seems to have won the heart of his opponent, even if it did not modify his views. M. de Jacobis appears to have been immensely impressed by the enormous benefits to Catholicity which must arise from the universality of steamboats in these days; he speaks of it as even of greater benefit to the missioner than the art of printing, " as the one," he said, " can only bring men together by the medium of the dumb language of books, and the other brings them into that personal contact which vivifies both heart and mind." On their arrival at Alexandria, the Abyssinians came to implore him to take them on to Jerusalem. The words of the Holy Father decided him to grant their request; for at M. de Jacobis' last audience the Pope had said to him, " Take them yourself, if you can, to visit the Holy Places, which will confirm them in all truth, and prevent their falling into bad hands." So the 4th of November found them at Jaffa, after having experienced the greatest kindness from the consuls at both ports. " I have taken the opportunity," writes M. de Jacobis, " to point out to our Abyssinians the wonderful love which springs from our holy faith, and which no other religion produces. They owned it several times, saying, 'it seemed to be the source of all charity.'

Oh, in how many different ways people, if they will, may become the apostles of souls!"

It will be needless to give to our readers many details of that visit to Jerusalem, a pilgrimage so marvellous in the effects it produces on all earnest minds, and coming, therefore, with redoubled power on a soul so holy and united with our Lord as that of M. de Jacobis. He was able to vindicate the rights of his Abyssinian people to be received free of cost by the Armenians, to whom they had sold their portion of the Church of the Holy Sepulchre for that very object, but which contract had been hitherto looked upon as a dead letter. He celebrated the Holy Sacrifice on the Altar of the Manger with the tears which such services draw even from the coldest hearts—the words, *Hic de Virgine Mariâ Jesus Christus natus est*, seeming to be engraved on one's mind in as strong relief as in the silver medal which the lips of the faithful keep ever bright! But his reflections on Jerusalem are too lucid and original not to be worth inserting here.

"Jerusalem, in the midst of the darkness with which she is overwhelmed, can never cease to be the City of the Soul. If you wish for a commercial capital, seek it in London; if for one where refinement and luxury and elegance combine, go to Paris. In Rome, you will find the faithful depositary of the treasures of Revelation. Other cities have likewise received special gifts. But Jerusalem, overwhelmed though she be, for the time, with the maledictions of centuries—Jerusalem must ever be the centre of all the great religious questions which have agitated the world. It seems to be her destiny that she shall sing to the end of time alternately the *Benedictus qui venit* and the *Crucifigatur* of the incarnate Wisdom. She is become, by no human institution, but by the sole will of God, the greatest religious university of the world. The Mussulman comes here, attracted by Omar's mosque. The tombs of the patriarchs, and prophecies but partially understood, gather together to this one spot Jews from every nation under heaven ; while Christians from the Atlantic to the Pacific, from the shores of Siberia to those of the torrid zone, equally press onward towards the glorious Sepulchre where their Lord was laid. A long series of events, overruled by the mysterious designs of Providence, convokes, by secret and various springs, every form of belief in the universe as to a General Council at Jerusalem. And that this is the work of Him in whose Hands are the hearts of men is so clear, that even the Mussulman, with his bitter hatred and in- tolerance towards the Christian name, sheathes his sword, and grants a safe-conduct to all nations and people who wish to worship here. And so it is again that here the rival sects, in bitter opposition to the one true and Catholic faith, endeavour to outdo one another in jugglery and imposture; and the pilgrims, often the most simple and devout of their race—Russians, Moldavians, Armenians, Syrians, Abyssinians, Copts, Greeks, and the like—deceived by the number of sanctuaries professed by their co-religionists, or duped by the sacred fire, return to their own land, only to propagate the errors and the heresy they have learned: and so the scandal of Jerusalem spreads over the whole world. Those who are zealous for the progress of Catholicism in the East ought never to relax in their endeavours to combat these fatal influences. Madame Véronique de Bavière is now striving to establish schools for the higher classes of both sexes at Jerusalem. It is only education which can remedy the evil, and that she has understood better than most politicians. It is the only lever which can raise nations to understand their higher destiny. Well will it be for the guardians of the Holy Places, already so respected and beloved, and to the shelter of whose convent *alone* the Turks, when alarmed by popular tumults, will confide their wives and children,—well will it be if these holy Franciscans will take the lead in a movement so essential to the times in which we live, and, by gaining public opinion to the cause of liberal yet Catholic education, regenerate the people, and pave the way for a new order of things and a purer faith among the nations of the earth."

On the 15th December, M. de Jacobis and his faithful Abyssinians left Jerusalem, and, passing by Gaza, followed the course probably taken by St. Joseph and the Virgin Mother on their flight with the Infant Saviour into Egypt. And so they arrived (across what is called the short Desert), after thirty days' march, at Cairo; and on the 14th of February 1842 the caravan started once more, and took the road homeward to Abyssinia.

M. de Jacobis, writing of their departure from Cairo, says : " Nothing could be more edifying than the sight of the convent of the Franciscan Fathers at Cairo at the time when we partook of their hospitality. Bishops and priests from the most distant missions were gathered together round their table. Some were bound for Ethiopia and the Bari mission, others for China and the Indies, to fill up the gaps left by their martyred brethren ; all were animated with the same burning zeal to shed their blood for the propagation of the faith. Eating, living, praying together, as we did, never did I more thoroughly realise the words of the Psalmist, *Ecce quam bonum et quam jucundum habitare fratres in unum.* Alas ! this joy was of short duration ; for the missionary's life is that of one who sows in tears : *Euntes, ibant et flebant.* One morning, ten of us started from those hospitable walls : six for China (among whom four were Italians, and the two others Chinese, brought up at the Chinese College at

Naples, which was founded by the celebrated Matthew
Ripa); and four of us for Abyssinia, including M.
Biancheri (an Abyssinian who had been ordained
priest, and given to us by the Propaganda), the
Brother Abatini, and myself. On taking leave of each
other, we wished one another but one thing: the
triumph of the faith of Jesus Christ, and the salvation
of souls. *Euntes, docete omnes gentes.*

" I feel that if the Abyssinian mission has of late
been so sterile, it is because it has not been watered
for a long time by the blood of martyrs. They tell
me that I shall obtain permission now to build Catholic churches, but that relics of martyrs will be wanted
for our altars. Sometimes I cannot help flattering
myself that I may be allowed to be of that number ;
but then the thought of my unworthiness deprives
me of the hope—the martyr's crown can only be the
reward of great sanctity.

" We took the way of the Desert of Suez, hiring
our camels of an Arab tribe named Antouni. The
English have established little station-houses every
two or three leagues along the road, for the accommodation of travellers ; but these hostelries require
a golden key, which did not suit a missionary's
finances. We had a small tent ; but one of our party
being sick, we gave it up to him, and slept ourselves
very comfortably on the sand, *à la belle étoile.* After
four days and four nights, we arrived at Suez ; the

fine rugged mountain of Whebbé, which stretches down to the sea, appearing as if on fire in the setting sun. In the harbour rode Mehemet Ali's one steamer, and also an English vessel bound for Bombay, which was to convey our Chinese missionaries so far towards the scene of their future labours. I could not help feeling that probably we should never again hear, in this world, of these our dear brethren and fellow-workers. No European newspaper is likely to make mention of their names. They will write about a dancer or a *prima donna*, and prostitute the name of a ' divine' creature in her honour. But of these men, leading the lives of angels—these men, who are about to give themselves body and soul for our Lord's work—no one will ever hear, or know, or care! *O curvæ in terris animæ, et cœlestium inanes!* The next day, Suez witnessed another triumph of Catholic charity — the arrival of a little colony of religious, Sisters of Jesus, who were on their way, with the Abbé Caffarel, to open a school for the education of children at Agra, in the East Indies. They had suffered much in crossing the deserts, having been surprised by the simoom; and being unable to manage their mules, they had run the greatest possible risk of their lives. We left Suez the next morning with these six ladies, but in different boats. Bruce speaks of the discomfort of these Arab barks, which are generally so heavily laden with corn that,

the sea-water entering through the disjointed planks
and swelling the wheat, the boats sink from sheer
weight, without wind or tempest. In such a wretched
worn-out tub did we embark, and M. Biancheri ex-
changed his berth for one on board of that which
held the nuns. But I stayed with our poor Abyssinians, who wanted reassuring. At Jambo, where
we came into the torrid zone, we met a crowd of
Hadjis returning from Mecca. Lying on wretched
mats, sickly, covered with vermin, and half-starved,
no sooner did they see the green flag which promised
them a speedy return to their own land, than they
rushed upon the deck of the little schooner, regard-
less of the blows from the janissaries who were
endeavouring to keep them back. Only a portion
could be crammed into the ship, and the rest returned discouraged, to wait for the next opportunity.
Seeing how this, the most solemn act of Mahometan
worship, is now held in discredit among the people,
one could not but feel that the last hour of the Koran
was at hand.

" On the 21st March we came into the harbour of
Djedda. There I found M. Sapeto, who had been
compelled by illness to leave Abyssinia. The nearer
we approached to Massouah, the more contradictory
and uncomfortable were the accounts of the state of
our mission. At last I received a letter from our good
Doctor Schimper, who gave me the following details.

"Oubié, the King of Tigré, had conspired against
the King of Gondar, Ras-Aly. He had forced the
new *Abouna*, or Bishop, to join him: the Abouna
Salama did not wish to be mixed up in the quarrel,
but Oubié had answered him : ' The only difference between you and my other slaves is the enormous price I paid for you in Cairo !' and so compelled him to accompany him. The rival kings met
in battle, and the fate of the day was about to be
decided in favour of Oubié, when, by a sudden
and unexpected flank movement, his tent was surrounded by a detachment of Gallas cavalry, and he
and the Bishop were made prisoners. Such being
the state of things, I resolved to leave M. Biancheri
in the neighbourhood of Massouah with Don Cyrillo ;
and I and the Frère Abatini continued our march
with the Abyssinian deputies to Oubié's country. It
was impossible to say what would happen to us, or
whether we should be able to do any good when we
arrived ; but it was clearly a duty to endeavour to
return, and not lose the fruit of our European journey. Our deputies had now all declared themselves to
be both Catholic and Roman ; and we had been able,
with a portable altar, to have daily Mass : so that
there was every thing to hope for, if they could return
to their own country in such good dispositions."

A little later he writes :

" I am, at last, arrived, and hasten to give you

an account of our long and perilous journey. There
were two routes, which equally led to the centre of
my mission—that of Dexa and that of Galaguora. I
chose the latter, as being safer. The former passes
across the desert of Samahar to the mountain of Taranta, as this St. Bernard of the Ethiopian Alps is
called. I had taken this route on my first arrival in
Abyssinia, and beheld that singular phenomenon by
which this chain of mountains forms, as it were, an
insuperable barrier between the two seasons—perpetual sunshine and incessant rain alternating every
six months on the opposite sides of the range.

" Our route by Galaguora was equally striking.
After leaving Laguaja, we found ourselves as in a
labyrinth of mountains, the blackened cones and cra-
ters of which gave evidence of their volcanic origin.
In one of the gorges, the good Frère Abatini was
startled by the appearance of a fine lion; but he
disappeared on our approach, and all I saw was a
multitude of gazelles feeding in the valleys. After
a four hours' march, we came on a stream in a little
valley, where a whole army of monkeys were gathered
together, both small and large. They screamed frightfully when we attempted to make a halt, and, retiring
to the lower spurs of the hills around, effectually succeeded in making us feel that we were intruders on
their domains. The next day brought us a succession
of misfortunes. The Naib of Arkiko, on a pretended

dispute as to the right of passage, made us pay heavily for our safe-conduct through his dominions; then four of our mules fell sick and died in a few hours of some unknown epidemic; the four that remained were already insufficient for the baggage, and were, moreover, needed for such of our party as were too ill and fatigued to continue their march. Altogether, any one coming unexpectedly on our sickly caravan would have imagined that we were the ambulance-wing of an invalided regiment.

"Towards night, our provisions were as completely exhausted as our strength. We were obliged to lie down fasting, with no beds but a mat laid on the stones, with the additional terror of the wild beasts, whom the carcasses of the dead mules had already attracted to our encampment. It was a terrible night; and, to add to our misfortunes, the black clouds began to gather ominously round us, and a heavy tropical rain drenched our clothes and put out our fire. As sleeping on these hard rocks, and in this condition, was impossible, I resolved to precede my companions, and resumed my march. How vividly, in the midst of a vast solitude like this, does one realise the greatness and presence of God! Full of thoughts of Him and of the mercy which had followed me ever since (thirteen months before) I had begun this Abyssinian mission, I climbed the hill, forgetful of fatigue, amidst the harmony of thousands.

of singing birds, and in an atmosphere embalmed
with jessamine, sweet acacia, and other flowering
shrubs.   As I walked on, I heard a step behind me,
and, turning round, found a monk of Gondar who had
been with me in Egypt and at Rome, Abba Gebra
Tensaite by name; and who had been cured of a
frightful fever in Jerusalem, where I had adminis-
tered to him the last Sacraments.   He had come to
implore me to allow him to remain with me, as he
thought his cure had been miraculous.   I told him
that, in the present state of things in the Tigré
country, I did not know if I should find even a roof
to cover my head ; but that if he would throw in his
lot with mine, I would share with him my bed and
my last bit of bread, and we would labour together
for our Lord.   He was overjoyed, and followed me
gaily and gladly along the stony and precipitous
track.   All those who were with me at Rome seem
to be filled with the same spirit—they only burn to
become apostles in their own country ; and fervent
hearts of this sort, under the direction of the mission,
is the one object I have had most at heart.   At the
same time, the Abyssinian people are proverbially
insincere.   The words of the Père Lobo were always
recurring to my memory : ' The moment an Abyssinian shows you great affection, be assured he has
determined to compass your ruin.'   So, was I or was
I not to believe in the protestations of my monkish

friend? After mature reflection, I resolved to trust; and the result proved that I was right in following simply the dictates of my own heart.

"Towards evening we reached Waha-Negus, the most beautiful spot which heart of painter could conceive. I never saw such flowers and plants: mimosas of enormous height, and other tropical shrubs; while the birds' notes had a sweetness which I had never before heard in any country. Yet this was in the heart of an enormous desert, rarely, if ever, visited by a human footstep. How miserable are man's conceptions in the face of God's works! We could hardly tear ourselves from this enchanting spot to toil up the steep mountain-ridge which separates the desert of Samahar from the pasture-lands on the opposite side, inhabited by a nomad and shepherd people called the Chohos. The bitter cold and the hardness of our couches roused us early on the 2d of May, and we were thankful to come down into the valley of Rerié-Malé, which village we reached towards midday.

"In going from this desert of Samahar to Adoua, the mission-station to which we were bound, the course is straight from north to south. Here a young Scotchman met me, a Mr. Bell, bearing letters from the mission; and with him came the boy who had cried so bitterly at my departure, and who was almost beside himself with joy at seeing me again.

The news they brought was favourable. Oubié had expressed great joy at the prospect of my return, and his people were ready to receive me with open arms. The next day we crossed the mountain called Wamba, camping afterwards in a fertile valley, by the side of a rushing stream, under the shade of a gigantic tree, called *mefleh*, and which is exactly like a citron or lime in flower and leaf. On the 4th of May we arrived in Caikor, the first Christian province on the frontiers of Tigré. The mountain which separates the two countries towers above one's head in colossal proportions, and a rent in the rocks appears to afford a passage, cut in squared stones, seeming as if created by human workmanship or by the force of artillery— till the gigantic size of each stone, and the enormous masses of granite standing up on either side of the narrow passage, make one realise a Power above that of man. Caikor is a rich and magnificent plain, watered by rivers, and entirely surrounded by an amphitheatre of hills. Elephants and lions abound, and we saw their traces every where. The hospitality of the people was remarkable, and made us feel instantly that we had entered a Christian country, although these poor people retain little of Christianity but the name.* Men, women, and children came out to

---

* Châteaubriand says truly: "Whenever you see on a door a cross or a picture of the Blessed Virgin, enter without fear; there you are sure to be well received."

meet the 'Abouna Jacob,' as they called me, although
the said 'Abouna' appeared among them with no other
clothing than a poor and dirty cloth. They brought
us a sheep, with abundance of milk and bread, and did
every thing they could to express their joy at our arrival.
I learnt, however, at this place, that the Copt 'Abouna'
was intriguing right and left to prevent my return to
Adoua, and had secretly sent emissaries to rob me
on the way. Hardly had we left Galaguora, than we
were attacked by a body of armed men on horseback,
who endeavoured to seize one of the baggage-mules.
I resisted, and spoke with such authority of my
friendship for Oubié, and the punishment which would
follow on any wrong being inflicted either on me or
on his deputies, that the villains were intimidated
and left us in peace. Then came up the governor
of Galaguora, who had been equally bribed by the
Abouna, and who tried to extort money from me on
various pretexts, in which he was foiled, and had to
retreat without having been able to gratify his avarice.
On the 6th May we arrived at Gouda-Falasié, where
we found the whole population engaged in celebrating
the nativity of the Blessed Virgin, which is fixed for
that day in the Ethiopian calendar, being the first
Sunday after Easter. But this feast, like all others
in this unhappy land, has more the character of a
pagan saturnalia than any thing else. The women go
out of their huts carrying their little children on their

shoulders, and holding in their hands a vessel filled
with a soup called *fit-fitò;* when they meet a man
in the street, they throw the contents of this vessel
over their heads, which is followed by scenes of
romping immodesty impossible to detail. It was still
worse with the young girls, the queen of whom, riding
on a mule gaily caparisoned, entered every young man's
house, followed by a whole tribe, claiming presents of
honey, cakes, and delicacies of all kinds; having con-
sumed which, the most indelicate dances followed. The
whole exhibition was horrible to the heart of a Christian priest, and it was with the greatest relief that we
left this scene of debauchery to continue our route. We
encountered continual annoyances from the emissaries
of the Abouna, but God overruled all things for our
safety; and on Thursday, the 13th of May, we arrived
at Mariam-Senito, where we found a whole cavalcade
of mules, with a crowd of our old Abyssinian friends,
who had come to meet us and conduct us in great
state to Adoua. And here we found every thing
to encourage us for the future. Every where the
Catholic spirit seems inclined to revive—the well-
disposed among the people of all classes are disgusted
with the liberty and license permitted by the different
sects, and wish for a return to a purer faith. The
kings themselves are favourable to us. Oubié, though
still nominally a prisoner, has been kindly and gener-
ously assisted by his rival Ras-Aly, who gave him his

liberty on parole, and will probably soon allow him
to return to his own country.

"Balgada, the governor of these provinces, has
begged us to come and preach to his people. The
Etchégué, who is at the head of the monastic orders,
has openly declared his veneration for our faith, and
his desire to reform the religious houses. Oubié,
who is far-sighted as a politician, thinks that our
ministry may be of use in raising the tone of his
people and securing the alliance of France; Ras pro-
tects us at Gondar; and the wisest of Ethiopian petty
kings, Sahala Salassié, has given evidence of the most
friendly feelings towards the mission. But, above all,
in the hearts of the people themselves, the seed sown
is beginning to bear fruit. The descriptions of Rome,
spread on all sides by the deputies on their return,
have dissipated a host of prejudices; and, finally,
Catholicism—which, for many centuries, has been
repudiated as the most criminal of heresies—now
enjoys an equal liberty with the other religions
established in the country. This alone is an immense
point gained."

For fear of wearying our readers, we pass over
the recital of our fervent missionary's labours during
the ensuing two years. The conversions recorded in
his journal are almost innumerable, and some of great
importance in a political point of view. Among the
latter was the granddaughter of the Emperor Tecla-

Ghiorghis—who, having been carried off by a powerful
Mahometan prince, had become a Mussulman, to the
consternation of the whole Abyssinian people. Being
unable himself to obtain access to the princess,
M. de Jacobis induced one of her ladies-in-waiting—
who was one of his earlier converts—to bring before
her the heinousness of her offence; and this was
done with such good effect, that the princess and
all her slaves were induced to abjure their apostasy
and be reconciled to the Church. This conversion
had a great effect on the whole court, and induced
many others to follow the princess's example. But
that of Dr. Schimper was even more remarkable.
He was a clever German naturalist, sent to Abyssinia
by the Society of Natural History at Wurzburg—a
man of great ability, of indefatigable research, and
universally beloved for his charity towards every one
with whom he came in contact. Received by M. de
Jacobis into the Church, he soon after married an
Abyssinian Catholic lady of eminent piety, and
thereby set the example—so much needed in Abyssinia—of a model Christian marriage and household.
They became afterwards the mainstay of the mission,
and the founders of the Catholic college which was
to crown the hopes of M. de Jacobis, and render his
work permanent in Abyssinia.

During this time, Oubié, having made peace with
Ras-Aly, returned victorious to his own kingdom.

M. de Jacobis went to meet him at Augié, where his camp had been pitched for the winter, and, in writing of this visit, speaks on a point to which present circumstances give a peculiar interest :

"I cannot help telling you something of those curious natural prodigies, called ' Amba' in the Ethiopian language, which seem to have been created by Providence to arrest the wars which otherwise might devastate this fertile country. An ' Amba' is a mountain which might have given the idea of the castles built for defence in other countries in olden times. These enormous masses of ferruginous stone are crowned at the summit by a square plateau, from whence the whole country round is, of course, visible ; and the sides of these mountains are regularly and sharply cut all round, leaving, amidst the precipices which defy any attempt at scaling them, only one narrow passage—capable of being defended by two or three men against a whole army. We tried to ascend the Amba Barbari (the mountain of Red Pepper), one of the most remarkable in the country, when some peasants, armed with only a few stones, forbade our attempting it; and we instantly saw that we had no alternative but to retrace our steps. With such natural fortresses, this country is simply impregnable ; and no European troops would have a hope of success."

Soon after, M. de Jacobis had the joy of seeing the wish of his heart accomplished, through the gift

made to M. Schimper, by King Oubié, of Antitchio, a
magnificent district in the most fertile part of Abyssinia, to build a college, and form the centre of the
Catholic missions throughout the country.   Oubié
made a solemn grant of this territory to the Catholics, and enacted that it should be exempt from all
taxes and freed from the passage of all troops.   This
property included thirteen villages and upwards of
4000 inhabitants.   M. de Jacobis started at once
to visit the country, and to choose a site for the
foundation of the new college.   The only allusion
he makes in his letters at this time to the hardships
he underwent in these journeys is contained in the
following passage : " I wish I could send you more
details of this glorious and beautiful country, this
perfect Eden for produce of all kinds, which the
mercy of God has awarded to our infant Catholic
colony. But it is impossible for me to work or write
for long together in this the hottest known climate
in the world, and that in the month of July."   In
spite, however, of this modest assertion, we find—in a
letter to N. T. H. Père Etienne, on the subject of the
college which his indefatigable zeal and energy had
just completed—that he had, with incredible labour,
written a series of catechisms in the three principal
languages of Abyssinia—the *Gheez*, the *Amaric*, and the
Tigré—dialects which in themselves present an almost
hopeless obstacle to Europeans ; and also a book

refuting the numerous errors which had crept into
the Abyssinian faith, with a lucid exposition of the
Catholic religion, confirmed by proofs drawn from
their own Sacred Scriptures. The avidity with which
these books were devoured by gentle and simple was
an abundant recompense to our holy missionary for
the almost insuperable difficulties, to say nothing of
the exhausting labour, of the undertaking.

In order to understand better M. de Jacobis'
Journal, we will here mention that the year in
Abyssinia is divided into thirteen months, of which
twelve have thirty days each, and the thirteenth,
called *pagmen* or *coogmen*, has only five days in ordinary years, and six in leap year. This month is
looked upon as the close of the year, like the month
of December in England, except that it is placed in
the time of the autumn equinoxes, instead of during
the winter solstice.

One day is especially marked in all Abyssinian
calendars; and that is the feast of St. John the Bap-
tist, being the close of the rainy season. The same
ceremonies take place as on New-Year's Day at Paris.
Friends and relations visit and make presents to
one another; subalterns give their superior officers
bouquets, and the officers, again, bestow more valuable
gifts: these are called, in the language of the country,
Anquetatache.

CHAPTER IV.

The Abyssinian monasteries—Progress of the mission.

THE most noble remains of Christianity still existing in Abyssinia are the monasteries. Here are still preserved those treasures of Ms. in Ethiopian and other languages to which every day gives greater value and importance. M. de Jacobis described his visit to some of these establishments in a letter to his old friend M. de Spaccapietra.

" There exists in Abyssinia, as I have before mentioned, a succession of mountains, often eleven or twelve thousand feet above the level of the sea, the ascent of which is only by a steep, stony, and narrow path, often mysteriously hidden in the folds of the ravines which cover their rugged sides. On the summit of hills like these, the convents are invariably placed,—partly as sanctuaries in case of danger, but also with the additional advantage of the perfect quiet and absence from worldly turmoil, so essential to monastic life. I was anxious to visit these monasteries, which are perched on the frontiers of the country as if to act as its bulwarks and lighthouses in the midst of the flood of paganism which threatens to overwhelm the country.

"The first I attempted was that of Damo. The 'Amba' which forms its pedestal is a magnificent mountain of white quartz, out of the shelves of which spring forth the most glorious flowering shrubs, especially the *quelqual*, a kind of euphorbia, and a singular variety, growing in the shape of an enormous chandelier. This plant is as characteristic of Abyssinia as the palm is of Egypt, growing every where in the greatest luxuriance.

"The river Najoc washes the base of this mountain, which is wonderfully fertile; and from thence a precipitous path led up to a gigantic rock standing out from the hill like a fortified bastion,—when the track seemed suddenly and unaccountably to lose itself and disappear. This rock formed the *clôture* of a convent of Abyssinian nuns who have the care of a little sanctuary hard by, which is a favourite place of pilgrimage to the devouter portion of the peasants. The superior came to speak to us from the other side of the enclosure, which Nature certainly has made next to impregnable,—but said that they were never allowed to ascend to the hermitage above, to which there was apparently not even a goat-track.

"Looking up, however, I perceived, as at Mount Sinai, two ropes hanging from a projecting point in the rugged cliff above my head; and this, evidently, was the only means of access to that which had become to me so great an object of interest and curi-

osity. After some hesitation, from the evident peril
of the undertaking, I made the monks above understand my wish to ascend. The ropes were lowered,
and behold me dangling in mid-air, bumping first
against one rock, then against the other, and with
difficulty keeping my head free from the dizziness
which this aeronautic proceeding entailed. When the
monks had safely landed me, and I could find breath
to look round and thank them for their timely assistance, I found myself on a plateau of about 2000
feet in width, of no great depth of soil, but still
susceptible of careful cultivation,—thus giving it the
appearance of a garden suspended between heaven
and earth. Olive, juniper, and sycamore trees, over-
hanging the precipice, shaded the little cemetery on
the right. After going over the monastery, I visited
the church, built out of the ruins of a sanctuary destroyed in the fifteenth century by Gragne, the Attila
of Abyssinia. At a glance I saw that the architect
must have been a European, both from the nature of
the plan and from the absence of any Oriental character about the building. Close to the church are sunk
150 cisterns, arranged in a rectangular shape, and
supposed to have been the work of the Emperor
Caleb, in the fifth century. Further on, were the
grottoes of the hermits. A young monk took me to
the one where the famous Abouna Tecla-Haïmanot
spent his life of penitence and prayer. My age

prevented my being able to get into this grotto, which is almost inaccessible; but my guide swung himself up into the cave, and, speedily reappearing, produced an enormous stone which tradition affirms Tecla put on his head when he passed the night in prayer.

"Another of the cells presented fewer difficulties, and I scrambled in. On the rock, which had been hollowed out to serve as a bed, was the impression of a man's shoulders and back, supposed to have been miraculously left in the stone. 'Here,' said my guide, ' the holy father, Abouna Aragavvi, was praying, when our Lord Jesus Christ appeared to him and said, "Because thou hast been faithful to Me, I will show mercy to the souls of all that are buried here for thy sake." ' You can suppose that I did not believe the legend; but I hailed it as a vestige of faith, and of their trust in God's mercy and in the doctrine of the remission of sins.

"At Bizen, which was the next monastery. I visited, a confused mass of granite rocks heaped one upon the other, of colossal size, add to the savage nature of the hermitage. Exhausted by the fatigues of the ascent, and by a two days' fast, it was with difficulty that we dragged our limbs to the foot of a great wooden cross, the only specimen of the kind in Abyssinia, which marks the approach to the convent. This welcome sign seemed to give us fresh life; and after a short halt we crawled on, through a grove of olive and juniper, to the summit, passing by the usual fine cisterns, which, unfortunately, were dry, though cut in granite, and carefully lined with cement. Now the poor monks are dependent on rain-water for their supply, which is often stolen from them by the elephants, who scale their fortress during the night for that purpose.

" From the summit of this convent, all that part of Abyssinia which was once Christian lay stretched as in a map at one's feet; the ruins of fourteen churches, which formerly were dependent on this great monastery of Bizen, filled one's heart with sadness and sorrow. Mahometanism and idolatry have crushed out the Christianity from this beautiful and fertile district. I could not but feel the truth of the reflection of M. de Montalembert, that wherever the monastic orders have kept their faith pure, they have been the centres of religion and civilisation ; while their demoralisation has been invariably followed (as is so lamentably the case in the East) by a corresponding destruction of all faith and *morale* among the people. The evil, in this case, has reacted on its authors. Although the hermitage remains, it is virtually deserted, save by a handful of religious, who are scattered up and down the country ; so that it is only on occasions of great feasts that they meet for the celebration of the divine office. So this, which was formerly called the ' Holy

Mountain,' is nearly abandoned ; and the people's curse rises up to the heights from whence truth has ceased to descend.

" But the most interesting of all these convents is that of Guenda-Guendé, which we had reserved for the last of our excursions.

" On turning to the south-east, by the plain of Agamié, you come suddenly on the most fearful-looking mountain to be seen, I should think, on earth. I scarcely know how to describe it, except by trying to make you imagine a terrific explosion of molten metal, which, thrown up in a vertical jet of eight or nine thousand feet in height, pours down its liquid streams of lava right and left, which there harden and become of the colour of rusty iron. No dew from heaven or stream from earth irrigates its barren and pitiless sides, which are bereft of all vegetation, and stand out naked and brazen in the glare of the burning tropical sun. In a crevice, split by some convulsion of nature out of the flank of this terrible mountain, popular tradition affirms that a famous dragon lives, known by the name of Gabella. Until the monks, by prayer, had exorcised this monster, and forced him to remain in his den, young girls were constantly offered up by the superstitious peasantry to appease his wrath. Absurd as these legends are, they are universally believed in Abyssinia; and certainly the nature of the place, and the volcanic crater on

which the monastery is built, might give rise to many
such delusions. The great depth of the crater, the
sulphureous air you breathe, and the venomous
reptiles which swarm in the caves, entitle it to its
appellation, the 'Lake of Dragons.'

"Mamer Walda Ghiorghis, the present abbot of
this monastery, is a man of the finest instincts, and far
better educated than the monks in Abyssinia generally
are. The moment he heard of our arrival, he came
out in his abbot's dress, with his community, to
welcome us into his monastery. He covered the floor
of his church with rich carpets, and received us with
great ceremony, seated on a curule chair called a
'Wambar;' he is one of the few Abyssinians to whom
this privilege is awarded, and etiquette exacts that
he shall not leave it even in presence of the king.
To the right of the hall of audience, where we had
been received, repose the ashes of King Sabagadis
and his children. This wonderful man did not live to
fulfil all that was foreseen at the beginning of his
reign; and at the very moment when Balbi wrote
that 'his genius would raise Abyssinia to the position
of a great power,' Sabagadis, kneeling with the cross
in his hand, was receiving his death-wound from the
spear of a Gallas enemy. The most beautiful orna-
ments in the church of Guenda-Guendé are the gifts
of this wise and generous prince.

"The next day, we were introduced to the library

of the monastery, where there is the largest known collection of Abyssinian works. I discovered that this treasure-house contained all the books in the Gheez dialect which have ever been written. There is also a magnificent copy of the ' Summa Theologica,' so celebrated in Abyssinia under the name of *Hai-manuota Abau*, and which bears a most curious witness to the truth of the Catholic and Roman Church on the very points which modern heretics deny. There is, likewise, a very important passage on the Holy Ghost ' proceeding from the Father and the Son;' but at the word *Wawald* (*Filioque*), some modern hand has scratched out the text, without, however, having been able altogether to efface the original letters. But the happiest result of our visit was the conversion of the abbot Mamer Walda Ghiorghis himself and six of his monks, who, long ago convinced of the errors which had crept into the Abyssinian belief, only waited for an opportunity to abjure them, and declare themselves one with us. To silence the calumnies of our enemies, Ghiorghis did not hesitate to say to them, ' To combat the Catholics with any hopes of success, you must begin by leading the Christian lives they do.' The good abbot wished to be received at once, and only reasons of prudence induced me to postpone the event for a few months. His holy and ascetic life had caused him to be held in universal esteem by the Abyssinians—even apart from the perpetual fast which his position exacted. To explain this, I should mention that abstinence from flesh meat and strong drinks forms part of the rule of these monks; but in the universal laxity which has crept into their order, they have come to the conclusion that such a regimen is impossible to flesh and blood, and so have contrived a novel and almost comical way of evading it. In choosing a superior, they make him take an oath that he will observe to the letter the severe penitential rule and the rigorous fast enjoined by their order, on *behalf of the rest of the community.* So that, in fact, the abbot pays in his own person the debt due from all! The moment he has accepted these hard conditions, he is watched by one and all with never-ceasing vigilance, and the smallest infraction of the rule is visited by instant deposition from his high office.

" Before closing this letter, I will say one word of the public education of Abyssinia, which is exclusively confined to these convents; and which is very important, as bearing on the future state of this country.

"What in Europe we call school, or college, or university, is comprised here in the universal denomination of *Debra.* No *Debra* can be governed by a lay body— each must be attached to a church and convent; therefore, when you hear of Debra Damo, Debra Metemek, and the like, it signifies the college and convent of St. John, or whichever saint may be its patron. The

professors are priests, and generally monks; though
sometimes men called *Defteras*, or masters-laureate,
are selected by the emperor for special branches of
instruction. To these colleges, princes and people
equally come and share in the public instruction. It is
entirely gratuitous, and the maintenance of the professors rests with the *Debra*. The miserable pittance
awarded to them is four *amulié* a year (the *amulié*
being equivalent to half a dollar), and twenty-four
measures of wheat, of fifty pounds' weight.

"You can imagine, therefore, the misery in which
these poor doctors and professors live. But what is
still more incredible is the amount of privations to
which a young man will submit so as to reach the
higher grades of science. Without speaking of the
personal service, often of the most menial character,
rendered by the pupil to his master—a service, however, which their filial affection for their tutors seems
to make sweet and easy to them—the student leaves
his home and family, carrying on his back the sack of
pease or meal which is to be his whole subsistence
during his college term; and when that is exhausted,
his only resource is to beg in order to live. Add to this,
that the length of the course of study exacted is perfectly
despairing. The course embraces seven years consecrated to learning the *Ziema*, or chant of the Church;
nine years for the *Suasuo*, or grammar and dictionary
of the Gheez language; four for the *Kenié*, or poetry;

and ten for the *Quédusan-mezahft*, or sacred books of
the Old and New Testaments. Civil and canonical
law, astronomy, and history, are also included in the
course of instruction given; but few students have
the courage to embark in them. After all, this
labour results in little science save one—and that is
in their knowledge of the Sacred Scriptures. To the
study of them are due the noble inspirations, the
delicacy and charity, and the high principle, which
are still to be found among the most intelligent
of these people; and in this respect I have often
felt that a humble *Deftera* had more real knowledge
than the most learned professors in our European
schools."

We have already spoken of the establishment of
the infant Catholic colony on the eastern frontier of
Abyssinia, and of the progress which M. de Jacobis
was making towards the conversion of the people in
the kingdom of Tigré. But the fame of his personal
holiness had extended far beyond the regions under
the sway of King Oubié; and now, on all sides, came
petitions from the surrounding provinces—from the
Gallas tribes in the south, and from the Bogos in the
east, from the pastoral tribes of Irob, to the desert
of Khartoun : and the cry was ever the same as that
heard by the Apostle of old, " Come over to Mace-
donia and help us."

M. de Jacobis could not remain deaf to an appeal

which promised so great a harvest of souls, and in the
two following letters we shall see in what way the
infant Church was once more planted in those vast
regions, and the marvellous success which crowned
his labours.

On the 20th October 1845, he writes again to
M. Spaccapietra :

" Having confided the care of our little Catholic
colony in Tigré to M. Biancheri, I started with the
Frère Abatini, and one or two native priests, for our
new mission. Our road lay through the province of
Gondet, by the plain of Mareb—a district at this time
infested with lions and elephants. One of our party
implored my permission to take a gun, in case of any
misadventure from these wild beasts. ' In an evil
hour I consented, and reaped the bitter fruit of my
want of simple reliance on God's mercy, and my
folly in trusting to human instruments of defence.
After having crossed the burning valley of Mareb,
and ascended a precipitous mountain which rises
perpendicularly 4000 or 5000 feet above the level
of the sea, we descended into the fertile plain of
Sarawé. Our people, dying of thirst and overcome
with fatigue, hurried to quench their thirst at a
fountain springing out of a rock by the roadside ;
when, all of a sudden, the people of a neighbouring
village rushed out to forbid our approach to the
water in question. One of the natives, brandishing

the terrible *gunt* (an Abyssinian club with a knotted
head, which is their most formidable weapon), struck
out right and left among our people ; and in the
midst of this unexpected commotion, a sudden explosion was heard. The fatal gun, which had been
thrown as useless on the grass, had exploded, and the
discharge had passed through the leg of our dear old
friend and fellow-worker, the priest Melchisedeck !
The artery was severed, and, in spite of all our
efforts, he expired two hours later in our arms.
But this misfortune did not come alone. The people
through whose territory we were passing were divided
into two hostile tribes. As soon as they heard the
noise of the gun, they imagined it was a signal of attack,
and each party flew to arms. Seeing the dead body
of our poor friend, however, they changed their minds,
and believed that we were come to attack them in
their own country ; and so both parties combined
against us as against a common enemy. We began
to fear that they would exercise upon us the *lex
talionis*, which is in full force in this country ; but
so completely had the death of our friend overcome
us all, that it was almost with indifference that we
found ourselves roughly seized and thrust into a
horrible dungeon whilst awaiting the decision of
our judges. However, help came from an unexpected
quarter.

" When I first arrived in Abyssinia, I had traversed part of this country, and the inhabitants of a little town called Gouda-Falasié had shown me kindness, and guided me through a defile in the mountains to the residence of another tribe, formerly Christians, and named Candida. The whole of the desert of Sennaar seemed there as if stretched at our feet; while, at the conflux of two streams, the little island of Meroé remains, famous in ancient times as the cradle of Egyptian civilisation.

" The boa-constrictor abounds in this district. His prey is the antelope, or *agazen*, which he watches for at the river-banks, his tail curled round a tree, —the rest of his long body being undistinguishable from the colour of the earth, to which it assimilates; and then fascinating his victim with his eyes, which are of wonderful beauty, in a moment its whole body is engulfed in the monster's jaws. He takes eight days to digest a feast of this sort, when he vomits the bones of his prey; and at that time the natives are sometimes able to compass his destruction. But to return to my story.

" Whilst passing through this district, we came on the ruins of an old abbey, and the people said to me: ' Why not come and settle yourself here among us, and rebuild this convent? we will gladly make over to you the stream and the surrounding territory, and you could do what you pleased with it.' It was a tempting offer; but how accept it? Wishing to temporise, I replied : ' But why don't you begin by rebuilding your church, which was burnt by the enemies of Sabagadis ? I will gladly help you to begin it, provided you are not subjects of the Abouna Salama.' ' Help us to rebuild our church,' they exclaimed with joy, ' and we will have no other Abouna than the one you shall set over us.' This was no sooner said than done. We made plans, and with difficulty scraped together a few dollars ; every man put his shoulder to the wheel ; and in a few months a very decent church was completed, and dedicated to the Blessed Virgin. All this was known in the neighbourhood ; and as the dungeon into which we had been thrust was only a few miles from Gouda-Falasié, the news of our captivity rapidly spread, and a detachment of young men flew to our rescue. In the mean time, we had the consolation of giving some little instruction to the children who crowded round our prison, so that we almost forgot our chains ; and having been able to effect the cure of two or three sick people—one especially, in an almost miraculous manner—the current of public opinion began to turn in our favour.

"Then arrived the youth of Gouda-Falasié, and they made the day of our deliverance one of real triumph. Men, women, and children threw themselves at our feet, imploring the blessing of ' the founders of the church of Mary,' as they called us ; nor could they sufficiently express their sorrow for the bad treatment to which we had been exposed. From this place, where God had so marvellously protected us, we came to the village of Ad-Counci (or the Country of the Fleas!), in the province of Amazon ; and to the river Mareb, one of the supposed smaller sources of the Nile.

" From thence we arrived at the village of Wachi, which was to be a kind of head-quarters for our mission, and took possession of a long, low, smoky house which had been prepared for us, but which was redolent with the smell of goats, besides other nuisances. However, by dint of cleaning and purifying the rooms with the sweet-scented juniper, we managed to divide the space, and turn it into a little college, where community-life could be more or less maintained. I spent every spare moment in translating the large Catechism into Gheez, and also the Psalms, for the *Defteras*, or native doctors, who crowded round us for instruction. A knowledge of the language used in the sacred books of Abyssinia is absolutely essential to the Ethiopian missionary, from the passion of the people for theological discussions, and the controversies which are always the subjects of conversation.

" The peasantry of this and the surrounding villages were in great distress at the time of our arrival, owing to the raids which had been made amongst them by the defeated troops of Oubié, who had ravaged their homes, and carried fire and sword into this hitherto peaceful district.

" But we were not destined to remain long in our provisional college of Wachi. The tribe of Mensa claimed our promised visit ; so, in spite of the gloomy prognostications of our new converts, and discouraging accounts of the almost impassable nature of the roads, and the difficulty of finding water, we left the hill-country, and proceeded on our route towards the plain.

" I will say nothing of our equipment and personal appearance. A good coat in this country exposes a man to almost certain robbery, if not death. Our only chance was to go utterly unprovided with any thing. Generally a horse or mule carried the cow's skin which served as the missionary's bed, with the sack of flour and the bottle of water which formed his commissariat. But here these things were luxuries not to be thought of. With bare feet and head, a coarse bit of canvas on our shoulders, and a walking-stick with an iron point, we started on our expedition.

" At midnight we found ourselves descending into the plain of Mensa, which lay stretched 6000 feet below our feet. Our way led by frightful precipices, which the uncertain light of the moon rendered more alarming. The soil was painfully slippery, and forced us to look almost all the time at our feet ; but here and there we came on magnificent ravines of wild and

savage beauty which I have never seen equalled;
while, at other times, we looked down on valleys so
desolate that they seemed as if stricken by a curse.

" When we neared the village, our suite took a
martial attitude, winding their one garment round
their loins; and, with a buckler of elephant's hide and
a lance at rest, they proceeded, with quick and dignified steps, to the hut of Cantiba, the chief man of the
tribe.   Mensa was the abode of four thousand souls,
most of whom were shepherds; rough, wattled, cir-
cular cottages, surrounded by palisades of wood to
keep out the wild beasts, and with strange, grotesque
mausoleums in the centre, made up the village.
Lowering spear and buckler, Achillas, the head of
our little escort, entered Cantiba's dwelling. This
man was the descendant of the royal and sacred family
from whom emanated the whole Abyssinian race; but
nothing remains to them now save the hereditary
title.   He is small, but well proportioned, with a com-
plexion like that of an Italian. He is dignified in
manner; and his long white hair, well anointed with
cow's grease, fell on his neck and shoulders, and
added to his venerable appearance.

" Although our arrival was unexpected at that
time, he received me with great courtesy; but, after
a little conversation, said, ' My affairs will compel me
very soon to leave the country; and after I am gone,
there would be no safety for you: so that you had bet-

ter return to Wachi before my departure.' This was
a civil but decided way of getting rid of us. However,
I could not bear the idea of having come so far in
vain ; and so I went in and out among the people, to
see if I could not produce some religious impression.
Several of the women knelt to beg my blessing, and
then the children, as usual, crowded round me. En-
couraged by their questions, I opened my little store
of needles and pins and medals, and gave them some.
Then I entered into conversation with the elder ones,
and asked them if they had ever heard of Jesus. ' No,'
they replied ; ' we never heard His name before.'
Then I began to tell them His history ; and they
became at once engrossed by it, and, when I stopped,
exclaimed, ' But why must you go ?'—an expression
echoed by a man of venerable aspect, who had been
listening too, and who, I found, was the brother of
Cantiba. I replied to him : ' Because your brother
wishes it.' He answered : ' I am married, and to a
Mahometan ; but we want to become Catholics, and to
be baptised at once.' I began his instruction ; and, in
the middle of it, Cantiba came in. ' I have just held
a council,' he said, ' with the elders of our tribe, and
we bid you welcome. We want to be taught by you,
and to be baptised as soon as harvest is over ; the *doura*
is now ripe. If you cannot stay with us now, we
will come and fetch you a little later ; for we want
to become Christians.' Here was indeed a harvest

ready to our hand, for which to thank God and take courage.

"I found the people living in great misery. The most beautiful sites in the place are occupied by the tombs; which, with their cylindrical form, and the abundance of quartz in the stone from which they are constructed, have a very beautiful effect when seen from a distance. Their funerals are conducted with great pomp; dressed in black, and with dust on their heads, the hired mourners, or ' weeping women,' execute a dance round the bier, increasing in velocity like that of the dancing dervishes, until they drop from sheer exhaustion, and fall into the arms of the ' women of consolation,' as they are called, who receive them. They have no vestige of religion; the very knowledge of God seems to have deserted them, with the extinction of the Catholic faith; but God, in His mercy, has left them that one belief in the immortality of the soul which is, after all, the fundamental basis of Christianity, and that gives us a common ground on which to begin. The mausoleums out-top the houses as the pyramids did the palaces; an evidence of the same feeling and the same motive. Man repeats himself in every time and country. They have a curious custom relating to robbery, reminding one of the laws of the Spartans. When a theft (say of cattle) is committed, the suspected person is brought before the Ancients; if the theft be clearly proved, he is made to refund

the number of cows stolen, but receives a dollar for
each from the proprietor, to make him more careful in
future.

"From Mensa we went to the convent of Debra
Bizen, of which I have already spoken. The country
through which we passed was so beautiful, that I
could not resist stopping to sketch it. Do not be
surprised; in Abyssinia, the missionary learns to do
every thing,—to be mason, carpenter, and architect
one moment—butcher, baker, and cook, the next.
We won't say much of the excellence of the work, but
the best master upon earth is necessity. From Debra
Bizen we came down into the desert of Samahar,
and to the village of Emkoullou. Our steps pressed
the soil which, two centuries before, had been watered
by the blood of the confessors whom the impious
Fasilidas had given up to the barbarity of the Turks.
Two nights after, by a beautiful moonlight, in crossing
the desert, we came on a band of brigands. To attempt
to escape was impossible—the 'Bogos,' as they are
called, brandished their long lances, and surrounded us
on all sides. I could do nothing but simply commend
our little party to God's mercy, and prepare for death.
Suddenly Achillas's name was mentioned. He was
known to the band, who instantly lowered their spears,
and after a few words exclaimed, 'Fear nothing, we are
friends.' At Emkoullou we baptised several men of
the 'Gallas' tribe, transacted the affairs of our new

mission, and then went on to the province of Agamié, where, with the permission of the prince, Oubié, we had purchased a site for a church and presbytery—one of the most beautiful in the whole country. The air there is pure and delicious; a limpid stream rushes down the glen, which is well wooded and gives a grateful shade. After a few months' labour, shared in by the whole community, our little mission-house and chapel were completed and ready for the reception of twenty-four scholars. We have built another church on part of the property of the celebrated abbey of Guenda-Guendé, whose abbot earnestly desires to be reconciled to the Church, as well as his whole community, of whom six have already been received. Here I met my dear old friend M. Montuori, on his way from Khartoun—where he had founded the college—to Gondar, where he was about to purchase a site for the new mission in that town. On the road from Sennaar to Gondar, he came on a wood called the Wood of Lions. Bones scattered here and there, and one or two bodies partially devoured, made the party feel that it was rightly named. All of a sudden they heard the low and terrible roar of the king of beasts. The mule on which M. Montuori was mounted, mad with fright, turned right round, and faced the enemy. Not being able to hold him in, he had no alternative but to throw himself off, falling on his head with such violence that he was left for dead.

M. Blondel, consul-general of the King of the Belgians, nursed him with such care that he recovered—the mule alone falling a victim to the foe. Such are some of the perils of the missionary's life."

In a second letter, addressed to the same old friend, M. de Jacobis writes:

"I have great and cheering news to give you as regards our labours in this country since I last wrote. There is a great district in Abyssinia inhabited by a purely pastoral people called the Irob, but whose importance has been greatly increased since 1830, when a famous warrior of their tribe, named Sabagadis, conquered a large additional territory, and by his wisdom and justice acquired a great and deserved influence among the petty kings by whom he was surrounded. Among our students was a young man of this country named Tecla-Ghiorghis, a youth very much above the average in intellect and in assiduity in his studies, and who had been converted by Abba Ghebra Mikael, the most enlightened of all the Abyssinian monks. One day Tecla came to me and said, 'I know no tribe who would so gladly become Christian as mine.' These words struck me. I knew that Tecla's father, a man of great influence, had been converted by his son, and that he had offered to present me to his tribe, who were then assembled at Alitiena; so, looking upon this as a direct call from God, I started from our mission-house at Guala, and,

after a few days' march, found myself within the
confines of their territory. These Irobs, who also go
by the name of Chocos, had elected a venerable old
man named Zora as their chief, he having merited
in his youth the title of *Hannaïta*, or ' Invincible.'
Habla-Marian (the father of Tecla-Ghiorghis) having
given them notice of my arrival, I was introduced at
once to the senate, or council of the Ancients, and the
conference began. After I had spoken, the president
rose, and, speaking in the name of the whole assembly,
professed their faith in the holy Catholic and Roman
Church, declaring that henceforth it should be the
religion of their tribe; making over to me, as its
representative, the ruined churches which were in
their country, together with the land round them;
and promising obedience to any one whom I might
appoint to instruct their people in the faith.

" Thus, after about two hours, I suddenly found
myself pastor of an immense multitude of souls who
were eagerly crowding round me to be taught, and
who, I felt, would become the most important Christian colony in the country. For the Irobs are of an
ancient and noble race, and claim a direct Roman
origin. The smallest goatherd, if asked the meaning
of ' Irob,' will reply, without a moment's hesitation,
' *Irob malet Rom, malet naou*'—that is, ' Irob means
Roman, and nothing else.' Tradition declares that a
sister of Solomon's married a Roman, and from this

couple sprang Andrew, who was the ancestor of the tribe.

" They conquered all the surrounding petty states, and reduced them to the position of hewers of wood and drawers of water. Some of the latter, the Cazaites, remain, but much in the position of domestic slaves. Their country extends from the mountains of Abyssinia to the Indian Sea. They are divided into thirteen tribes, and are distinguished for their equestrian powers, so that the term '*Angolas afuas*'—or, 'horseman equal to an Angolas'—has become a proverb in Abyssinia. Some curious tombs are found scattered up and down the country, which appear neither to have a Christian nor a Mussulman origin. The latter are generally hollowed out of the rock, while the former are on the high roads; but these sepulchres date from the days of idolatry.

" The people themselves are little removed from pagans. When we began building our first mission-house and church at Alitiena, we were looking about for a favourable site, and pitched upon an eminence near a little wood just above the town. The guides, in terror, implored us to choose some other position. 'Why?' we asked. They then explained to us that this was the spot where yearly sacrifices were offered to *Ghinni*, the god, or geni of the fields, on whom their crops depended. Thinking it more than ever important to destroy this superstition, we continued our work, cutting down

the sacred trees of the grove; and when the people saw
that nothing disastrous happened in consequence, they
began to laugh at their own simplicity. They are
very much given to divination and magic. All those
who work in iron are called *bouda*, in the language
of the tribe, and are supposed to have the power of
turning themselves into hyenas, and to have endless
methods of procuring the death of their enemies. This
superstition entails occasionally serious consequences;
for let a man or a woman exclaim in the delirium of
fever that such or such a *bouda* is killing them, and the
family of the sick person will instantly rush to the
house of the unoffending worker in iron, and often
murder him on the spot. The women are the slaves
of the tribe. The young girls are invariably sold to
the highest bidder, be he Mussulman or Christian. If
they become widows, they are forced to marry the
younger brother of the defunct husband. Polygamy
is the fashion, even among those calling themselves
Christians—and, in fact, nothing can be more deplorable than the position of the latter.

"The priests, so called, are sunk in the lowest debauchery, and only make use of the people to extort
money. One day, Habtû, the brother of our chief, went
to one of these men to confession. He asked him first
for forty dollars. The poor man was thunderstruck.
' I have kept all the fasts,' he replied,—' Lent, Advent,
and the Assumption, besides other days; will not that

H

suffice to get me absolution?' 'Fasts are doubt-
less good,' replied this wolf in sheep's clothing, 'but
money is necessary before you can obtain pardon.'
The poor man paid the forty dollars, saying: 'Now,
then, father, give me absolution and communion.'
'The first, yes,' replied the priest; 'but for the
second you must ask some one else.' The same
story was repeated. The man was driven to despair;
he had not eighty dollars in the world. Finally, the
second priest was contented with twenty; and so
poor Habtû paid sixty dollars in order to perform
his ordinary Paschal duty! The melancholy thing
is, that it is not from ignorance of the nature of the
Sacrament that this horrible sacrilege takes place;
for the belief in the Real Presence is stronger in
Abyssinia than in any other country in the world.
A man will not spit for three days before and three
days after taking the Holy Communion; and were
it not for fear of disgusting you by the account of
their habits, I could give you several other instances
of their intense veneration for the Holy Eucharist.
Therefore, it needs but the advent of a pure and
holy priesthood to regenerate these people; only, the
missionary must be cautious not to offend their prejudices unnecessarily, and to win his way by patience,
charity, and forbearance; above all, he must entirely
forget his old habits, and live in the manner his
people do.

" In a few days, M. Biancheri and I are going
to start two rough tents made of sail-cloth, like the
native ones. Until now, we have crept into the little
dens or caverns which the shepherds use while guard-
ing their flocks ; or else slept in the wood huts of the
Irobs, which are made of boughs of juniper and sycamore : for the dwellings of the elders of the tribe
alone are constructed of mud and stone, with a mortar
of cow's dung. But, however miserable the Irob
habitations may be, there is no doubt about the cordiality of your reception ; their welcome goes straight
to one's heart. The best corner of the hut, the clean-
est cow-skin, is instantly placed at your disposal. It
is thus, cross-legged, that the missionary sits and
catechises his new converts ; not without, I must
own, sundry contortions in his efforts to catch the
vermin which swarm round him and about him, and
from which it is impossible to escape. The little instruction generally ends with prayer and the recita-
tion of the Rosary. Then we have supper ; which,
in honour of the missionary, becomes a solemn feast.
First, they bring the fattest goat and present it. I
go through the form of accepting it ; but then, knowing the poverty of these poor people, I intercede for
its life, and suggest that it should be reserved for a
more important occasion. Then they produce the
gonfo, which is a kind of soup of oat-flour swim-
ming in butter. Oat-cake is looked upon as a great

delicacy by the Irobs, for they never taste wheat.
This *gonfo* is served in a great bowl of sycamore-
wood, and is the only substitute for meat. Then the
women retire, for it is not the custom for their sex to
eat with their masters. The men, sitting in a half-
circle, set to work and devour this soup, having no
spoon but their hands, which they thrust into the
butter at every mouthful. This is the only thing
which never fails ; and when one flatters oneself that
one may eat the oat-cake alone, the master of the
house instantly pours in more butter from a little keg
which he holds in his hand. As king of the feast, I
ought to set the example on these occasions ; but I
confess to being unable to swallow it, and my guests
save me the trouble by finishing it in a few moments.
Then follows the *lahano-han*, a *sorbet* very much
liked by the Irobs, who drink it in what they call
a *dagonda*, a cup made of fine plaited straw, manufactured by the women. The plaiting of these vessels
is so close and even, that not a drop escapes. These
cups are of a cylindrical shape, and, with smoke and
dirt, are of the colour of ebony. When filled, the
natives take a burning brand from the hearth and
plunge it into the liquid, stirring it about till the
milk rises in a scum to the top, when it is handed
round to the company. Then the conversation begins
to get animated, and goes on increasing in noise and
vigour till the end of the feast. The supper over,

and evening prayers said, the missionary lies down
to sleep on his cow's skin, which he does as well as
the noise and the vermin will allow him. The natives
themselves sleep on the bare ground. As to their
dress, they formerly wore the white linen common
to the Indians, and which they called *berghella*;
but since the communications with the sea-shore
have been interrupted, they content themselves with
a kind of rough cloth made in Abyssinia, which they
pay for in kind ; that is, with the butter and honey
which abound in their country. As to the women,
on great festivals they wear a chemise and cloak
made of white linen ; but their ordinary dress is a
simple sack of coarse unbleached stuff, with a rough
hair-cloth cord to serve as a girdle round the waist.
This is for the married women. The *virgini*, as
they are universally called, have only a couple of
goat-skins with their black and shining hair, one of
which covers the loins, and the other is slightly
thrown over the shoulders, which it scarcely con-
ceals. Seen at a distance, all these people resemble
the old hermits of the deserts; and it is difficult to
distinguish one from the other.

" They are a brave and chivalrous race, quick to
feel and to resent an injury, but generous when their
anger is past. During the first six months we remained among them, a fierce quarrel took place
between two of the tribes, which it required great

prudence and tact to pacify. But after repeatedly
going from one camp of belligerents to the other, we
at last succeeded in bringing about a definative peace.

" This people excel in surgery, and give proof of
a skill and courage which are really amazing. As
an instance, one of our best friends in the tribe suffered from a malady in the intestines, for which they
have a peculiar remedy. He announced his intention
of performing the operation himself. He first filled
a wooden bowl with butter, which he covered with a
bladder, like a very fine net, of a cow recently killed.
Then, sitting down on the ground, he opened the
lower stomach with a razor, took out his intestines
and placed them in the net, which was still hot,
cleaning them, and placing them carefully back in
their proper place. He then sewed up the wound,
and, lying down on his back, took as little food as
possible till the wound was healed, and a complete
cure effected. They are kind and charitable in nursing the sick, and extremely hospitable to strangers.
One day when I was on my way to give the Viaticum
to a dying convert, I came on a tomb purporting to
be that of thirty young men. On inquiring the meaning of this, my guide told me that on this site there
was formerly a village renowned for hospitality. All
the idlers who preferred living upon other people to
working for their living, made it their home. The
villagers received them with the utmost kindness,

and supplied them even beyond their means. The consequences may be foreseen—the supply of food not being equal to the consumption, a famine ensued, and the people fell sick. At last only thirty remained, who were reduced to living skeletons. They were about to drink the last drop of milk which their rapacious guests had left them, when some fresh people knocked at their door and claimed their hospitality. 'What are we to do?' they exclaimed. 'If we drink the milk, our guests will go away fasting; if we do not drink it, we must die.' They chose the heroic part—received the strangers, gave them all they had, and then lay down and died. In acknowledgment of this wonderful and unheard-of act of self-sacrifice, this monument was erected by the neighbouring villagers.

"Some patience is required to bear with the minute examination of every thing belonging to you which is the consequence of these friendly and hospitable receptions. Nothing escapes their notice or their touch in your room or about your person; and having at last satisfied their curiosity, they lie down by your side and whistle in your ear the different tunes with which they lead their cattle to pasture or home again to milk; sometimes interrupting their whistling to break out into a song in praise of a favourite bullock or heifer, the names of these animals being carefully introduced. The music

ended, the Irob suddenly starts up and goes out
without ever wishing you good by. But trying
as these proceedings may be, there is a compensa-
tion for the little exercise of patience and temper
in the docility with which the people will follow
your instructions, and the good - will they show
on every occasion. The missionary needs far less
than this to induce him to overlook any amount of
apparent indiscretion.

" I have before mentioned the state of slavery in
which the women are kept. The moment a little girl
is born, she is promised in marriage to some one chosen
by her parents, and for a certain sum,—no matter how
repugnant the man may be to the poor girl herself
when she grows up. The first trial which I attended
when I arrived was on the question of a child having
been *fiancée* to two different people. It was ruled
that the mother was to decide which of the sons-in-
law she preferred. The two suitors in the mean time
remained as cold and indifferent as if it did not concern them. The choice made and the trial over, the
rivals embraced one another with every expression
of friendship, and seemed to care as little as if it were
a question of a sheep.

" News is conveyed among the Irobs in an original
but efficient manner. Carrier-pigeons, beacon-fires,
and the like, are the usual resources of a primitive
people. But here they have another and perhaps more

satisfactory method. By a law dating from the earliest
times, they claim the right to stop any passing traveller on the road, and to question him as to the current
news of the day or of the district through which he
has passed; and the said traveller is bound to satisfy
their curiosity to the full. In the same way, the
questioner is compelled to reply to any inquiries that
may be made by the passer-by, and to give him all
the local gossip of the place. This itinerant jour-
nalism, though inconvenient to a stranger, is very
valuable to the people of the country; and I am
bound to say, that in fidelity and exactness it greatly
surpasses the ordinary European newspapers, just as
the image reproduced on the looking-glass is more
faithful than any painted picture.

" Perhaps I shall weary you by my long descriptions of these tribes; but it is difficult to make you
understand otherwise the nature of our daily life.
You may, perhaps, exclaim, that a missionary's
existence among them has few compensations; but
I assure you it is far otherwise. Not to speak of
the spiritual joy of seeing so many souls brought
to the knowledge of our Lord, and the consolations
which God bestows on those who devote themselves
to an Apostolic life (of which I feel myself utterly unworthy), there are many material pleasures; as, for
instance, in the excessive beauty of the scenery and the
flowers, the luxury of fresh milk when one is thirsty,

and even the thick soups which one finds so delicious when fainting with hunger..

" But the good dispositions of the people, their gratitude and personal affection, are very cheering to the missionary's heart. Is it not edifying to see a little goatherd of seven or eight years old, to whom you have taken some pains to explain the catechism, holding a small class of children of his own age on the mountain-side, of his own accord; and then presiding, with wonderful recollection and piety, at the evening devotions of his family? or to see old men die in the holiest and best dispositions? or to receive entreaties from young men to be prepared for holy orders? I was very much touched one day at hearing a boy, when asked ' what he wished for most on earth,' reply, ' I wish that our dear father, whom God has sent us, may live as long as Abié (the Abyssinian Methuselah), so that, at the hour of my death, I may have the joy of receiving the last Sacraments from him, as my elder brother did, who died in his arms.'

" They are positively *greedy* for religious instruction ; from the little child of three years old, who can scarcely speak, to the old grandmother on whose knee he is sitting. It has moved me to tears to hear the old shepherds and the young soldiers on the hill-side reciting together the Rosary or the Litanies, the lowing of the cattle mingling with their voices, as if ' every thing that had breath' were ' praising God.' One day,

being asked to baptise a Cazaïte baby, I told the
father to bring it to the church at a certain time. I
went; but no baby appeared. I sent to know the
reason, and found that the baby was dying. Taking
the holy oils, I started off instantly to discover where
these people lived, and to perform the sacred function.
The Irobs tried to dissuade me, as it was in the dog-
days, and the road was infested with venomous serpents. Seeing I was determined, however, two young
men instantly volunteered to be my escort. Towards
evening, exhausted with fatigue, we reached the hut
in the mountains, and there dismal wailings met our
ears. ' O my God! then the child has died unbap-
tised!'—this was my first thought. I hastened my
steps, and rushed into the grotto, where I found
the child dying in the mother's arms. ' Quick to
the fountain!' I exclaimed; and seizing the first thing
that came to hand, which happened to be a wooden
bowl, I dragged the mother to the water, and there
had the joy of pouring on the poor little child's head,
while still living, the sacred waters of regeneration.

" Such are the joys of our life, dear and reverend
brother. I thank God that, in spite of my forty-six
years, I still have strength to climb these mountain-
sides, to be cheered by the sight of such faith, and to
preach our holy religion. The great difficulty we have
to contend with here is in the purchase of land for
churches and missions. Every acre belongs, not to

this or that individual, but to the district, or to the whole province. Therefore, to get so large a number of people to agree as to terms is next to impossible. However, God has turned the hearts of many towards us. Grants of land have been freely made, on many unexpected occasions, for these purposes; so that we must hope for a similar extension of our work throughout the country."

CHAPTER V.

IT was impossible that so small a number of workers should suffice for the evangelisation of this enormous country; and, at the earnest entreaty of M. de Jacobis, Monsignor Massaja and a body of Capuchin Fathers were appointed by the Holy See to the Gallas mission; M. Massaja being consecrated Bishop of Cassia, with powers of conferring holy orders throughout Abyssinia. This event, so important for the future welfare of the mission, is detailed in the following letter from Monsignor Massaja, which reveals, even more than his own words, the marvellous humility and sanctity of our holy missionary. He writes as follows:

"In the month of June 1846,—a date memorable from the death of Pope Gregory XVI.,—I started for the Gallas mission, to which the late Holy Father had appointed me. In order to meet the wish of the Vicar-Apostolic, M. de Jacobis,—who was most anxious to obtain the ordination of a large number of native converts whom he had prepared for the sacred ministry,—I took the route by the Red Sea and Massouah, instead of by the Nile, as I had originally intended, and arrived at this place about the middle of October. Massouah is the port of Abyssinia; but is nothing but a miserable collection of huts on a little barren island, under Turkish dominion. There is not a single stream or a blade of grass on this arid rock, and the heat is proportionally intense. I had both letters and money for M. de Jacobis; but, as he did not know of my intended arrival, I was very much surprised at finding two of his students waiting for me at Massouah. I inquired of the consul if any boats or messengers had come within the last few months who could have spread the report of my visit. He replied, that they had had no communication with Europe for more than eight months. I then questioned the two boys as to M. de Jacobis' reason for sending them to meet me. They replied, that the mission was reduced to very great straits for want of the supplies, which generally arrived earlier from France; and that one day, when they were in great distress at being unable to repay a sum which had been lent to them, M. de Jacobis, having made a longer act of thanksgiving than usual after Mass, rose and told them that God had heard their prayers, and sent them succour even beyond their hopes; and he then desired these two young men to start at once for Massouah, to be ready to receive me, and the supplies I should bring with me. It was, therefore, clearly known to

him by a revelation from God. The immense veneration with which the people at Massouah regarded him,
although they were Mussulmans, made me expect a
very remarkable person. I wrote instantly to announce
my arrival, and to send him his letters; on the receipt
of which missive, he started directly from his missionary college, and arrived at Massouah after eight days'
march. As soon as I heard he was come, I ran down
to the port, and there saw an Arab boat approaching,
filled with Abyssinians dressed in unbleached cloth,
with simple white turbans round their heads, and
with parasols made of a curious palm, unknown in
Europe; but I could not discover any European
among them. 'Where is M. de Jacobis?' I exclaimed.
Hardly had the words escaped me, when the smallest
and most poorly clad of the party, accompanied by
one of the students I have before mentioned, made
his way through the crowd of Arabs on the quay,
and threw himself at my feet, which he pressed and
kissed. This was M. de Jacobis! His intense humility, and that of the students he had brought with him,
who all knelt and kissed my feet, overwhelmed me
with confusion. I would fain have done the same to
him, had I not feared it would appear like a carica-
ture. I tried to raise and embrace him; but he drew
back as unworthy. The crowd, dumb with surprise,
watched this meeting, and made way for us to pass
together into the house. I wanted them to insist on

his sitting down by my side on my poor little Arab
bed; but he would not hear of it. He remained sitting
on the floor, with his students, at a modest and respect-
ful distance. I said to him, in our own language,
how distressed I was at this conduct on his part, and
implored him to recollect that he was a European like
myself, besides being Vicar-Apostolic, and, as such,
entitled to the same respect. His answer silenced
me, while it increased my admiration for his humility:
'Monsignor, you are the first real Bishop who has
appeared in this country. I know the idea these
people have of the dignity and position of a Bishop.
Let me act as I am doing, or I shall scandalise my
neophytes.' I had nothing left for it but to let him
have his own way, and to implore him to take charge
of my household and myself. From that moment, as
if by magic, our little party appeared transformed into
a religious community, living according to regular
rule, with fixed hours for prayer, study, and religious
exercises. We remained a fortnight at Massouah;
and, during that time, I never saw him a moment
idle, in spite of the intense heat: he was always either
praying, or teaching, or baptising, or confessing, or
translating religious works into the native dialects, of
which he was a complete master.

"In going from hence to Guala, it was the same
thing. During the eight days' march, the lessons
and spiritual exercises were never omitted. Another

thing surprised me extremely. Although it was now many years since he had left Europe, and many months since he had received any letters from home, or seen a newspaper, he never asked me for any European news. Once he wished to hear the details of the death of Gregory XVI., and of the election of Pius IX.; and then he spoke of Rome, and of the Congregation; but, except on that occasion, he never alluded to friends or country. It seemed as if he had none now but those of his adoption. His heart was in such complete union with God, that it appeared to make him forget every thing which did not concern His service and glory, and the welfare of his mission.

"The more I saw of him, the more I could only adore the inscrutable wisdom of God, who had chosen this man above all others, who was the very type of mortal perfection, of self-abnegation, purity, and almost divine humility, to convert a nation where all trace of these virtues had been lost in the most over-bearing arrogance and the grossest materialism and sensuality. Once I ventured to remonstrate with him about his dress, which was generally worse and more tattered than even that of the natives; for if he had a decent article of clothing, he invariably gave it away. He thanked me warmly for my 'kind advice,' as he called it, but replied, 'Monsignor, who should be the best dressed, the master or the servant? All I know is, that God, the Church, and my superiors,

I

have sent me here to be the servant of this nation. I
know nothing else.' On this principle he invariably
acted. He never would take a chair, or any food
differently prepared from the rest. Sometimes, when
he returned completely exhausted from some distant
sick-call, the lay brother would bring him something
a little more tempting or strengthening. He would
receive it with touching thankfulness, but then almost
immediately pass it on to another. On our journeys,
I have seen him continually give up his horse, or his
mule, or his parasol, or his cow's-skin bed, to one or
other of the priests or students, and insist on trudg-
ing on himself on foot, without the slightest protection
from the burning sun; and then sleeping on the bare
ground that another might rest more luxuriously. Nothing could have been more trying to a man's natural
pride than the first expedition he undertook on arriving in Abyssinia, when accompanying the deputies
to Cairo 'to buy the Coptic Bishop,' as the natives
expressed it. Abba Gabriel, a fervent Abyssinian
priest, told me that M. de Jacobis had spent eight days
in fasting, solitude, and prayer before undertaking
this most repugnant journey; but when once he had
resolved upon it, nothing could deter him. He spoke
to the deputies as follows: 'My brethren, the will of
your king, and still more the will of God, obliges me
to accompany you. I will do every thing in my power
to serve and be of use to you.' The deputies replied

with brutal insolence, ' You must clearly understand that you are to be our slave; and if you do not obey us, woe be to you!' Any one else would have given up the mission in a fury, and carried his complaint to the king. But M. de Jacobis, who, in his intense humility of heart, only desired to become really the slave of these people for Christ's sake, replied, ' You are right; look upon me as your slave. I will do my best to satisfy your wishes.' What he had promised, that he fulfilled to the letter. During that terrible three months' journey, he made himself truly, like his Divine Master, the servant of all; nursing them when sick, bearing with their continual insolence, preparing their food, washing their feet, carrying and fetching water, making their beds—performing, in fact, every possible menial office. The more he laboured, however, the more insolent and odious was their conduct towards him. They reviled him on every possible occasion—accused him even of treachery, and of an intention of selling them to the Turks — and added menaces and threats to their cruel words. He never answered again, except sometimes by a noble smile which had in it more of heaven than of earth. This lasted through the first part of the journey: by degrees, his unutterable patience, charity, and forbearance began to tell upon them. One by one, they began first to feel ashamed of their conduct, then to admire, and finally to defend him. The moment he found he was beginning to overcome their prejudices, he adroitly turned the conversation on questions relating to the faith, and insensibly interested them so much that, by the time they got to Cairo, two-thirds of the deputation were converted to the Catholic Church, and all of them were heartily ashamed of their previous disgraceful behaviour. So mightily did this great example of Christian humility prevail over these pagan hearts.

" At Guala, I had the consolation of ordaining a very large number of native priests, who had been most carefully prepared by M. de Jacobis. Their intense devotion and recollection astonished as much as it edified me. Previously I had held a confirmation which was doubly interesting to me from a good many of the Gallas tribe taking part in the sacred rite, the Gallas being the people to whom the Holy See had specially directed my steps. These converts were the fruits of the zeal of Mdme. de Goutin and of Mdlle. Mélanie, her eldest girl, who, with M. de Goutin—the French consul—have done so much for the honour of God in this country.

" About the end of June 1847, I received instructions from Rome to consecrate M. de Jacobis Bishop of Nilopolis and Apostolic Vicar of Abyssinia. He was at that time away, establishing his new priests in their different missions; but I forwarded to him the briefs from the Sacred College, and was much surprised at receiving no answer. Fearing the letters might have miscarried, I questioned the messenger. He replied, that M. de Jacobis had received them safely, but had appeared much troubled at their contents; and that one of the priests, coming in soon after, had found him on his knees and in tears. He added, ' he feared M. de Jacobis was ill.' I replied, 'He is ill with a rare disease, and that is over-humility.' Anxious, however, to obey my orders, I wrote to him to say that I had several serious matters on which to confer with him, and that I begged he would return at once to Guala. These few words were at once a command to him; and on their reception, leaving his dinner untouched, he started off instantly from Alitiena, and arrived towards evening, as we were sitting down to supper. As he appeared exhausted with fatigue and very sad, I said nothing that night; but the next morning, after Mass, I began, and conjured him in the name of the Pope to submit to the proposed consecration. Instead of listening to me, he threw himself on his knees before the altar, and began crying bitterly, accusing himself of all the sins and imperfections of his past life; and that with such profound conviction, that I found it impossible to make him hearken to reason. I gave it up, therefore, for the moment; but a little later returned to the charge, and, finding all entreaties in vain, adopted a tone of command, and showed him how his useless resistance increased the

difficulties of my own position, and compelled me to
delay indefinitely my arrival in my own diocese. On
my making this appeal, he remained perfectly still and
silent for a few moments, and I thought my point had
been gained. But I was mistaken. Throwing himself on his knees at my feet, he exclaimed, ' My
father, I hope that God will not look upon my dis-
obedience towards you as a sin, when it is to avert
that which would be the ruin of this mission, and the
disgrace of the episcopate. But, independently of my
own unworthiness, I belong to a Congregation, and I
could not take such a step, which, as it were, would
separate me from it, without being morally sure not
only of the permission of my superior-general, but
also of his formal commands. My body belongs to
him ; and although the Church is above my superior,
yet you know well that such a charge cannot be
imposed upon me without his consent. Lest, however, my refusal should place you in any difficulty at
Rome, I will give it you myself in writing.' Dis-
appointed and discouraged at this result, I left him
for my new diocese ; but, a year after, having heard
from Rome that great discontent had been expressed
at my failure in this matter, I returned again to
Massouah, and told him the reason. He begged for
eight days' consideration, which he spent in retreat,
having besought the prayers of all his missioners for
light and guidance. At the end of that time, I

received from him a most wonderful paper, in which
he repeated all the arguments he had previously used,
with the most exaggerated view of his own sins of
omission and commission—winding up with the
declaration that nothing should induce him to consent
to accept such a charge, unless it were by the positive
command of the Holy Father. This letter I still keep
as the most marvellous and almost incredible proof of
how, in the infinite wisdom of God, He permits souls
of such rare sanctity to remain plunged in the deepest
sense of their own unworthiness, lest their humility
should be endangered, and they lose thereby the full
lustre of their crown. I own I began then, for the
first time, to understand how great saints—those
whom God honours with extraordinary marks of His
favour—can believe themselves to be the greatest
sinners without a shadow of affectation or insincerity.
The nearer they are to God, and the more they understand His marvellous perfections and incomparable
sanctity, the more they realise their own imperfections,
invisible though they may be to the eyes of other men.
I have always preserved this paper of his as a great
treasure, and as a looking-glass in which I could behold my own infirmities, and gain strength and courage
when my weak and feeble heart was tempted to fall
into sloth or apathy. At the same time, his determination placed me in very great difficulties; and
I was beginning to despair of shaking his resolu-

tion, when Providence took the matter into its own hands.

" The Turkish government had taken possession of the island of Massouah in 1604, four years before the Portuguese entered Abyssinia to defend the people against their Mahometan invaders. The mainland belonged to Naib, chief of the Soho tribe, who had his residence at Arkico. He was a tributary king to the Abyssinian monarchs, from whom he received his investiture. In the month of February 1847, the Governor of Massouah, Ismaël Effendi, made war with the Naib, and took possession of Arkico and the sea-coast, building fortresses on the mainland to defend his position. The Naib appealed to his protector, King Oubié; and the latter determined to come down to the coast and make war with the Turks. In the mean time, all the population, subjects of or protected by the Turks, had to leave the mainland, and take refuge in the island. M. de Jacobis, for this same reason, was compelled to leave Emkoullou, and take refuge in Massouah. In the beginning of January 1848, the troops of Oubié came and massacred all the populations favourable to the Turks who remained on the sea-coast. M. de Goutin, who, as a friend of Prince Oubié's, and French consul, thought he might remain in safety at Emkoullou, ran the risk of being massacred with his family in his own house, while the French flag was torn down and burnt before his face.

The Mussulmans, seeing the havoc the Christian Abyssinians had wreaked on their co-religionists, threatened
to revenge themselves on Massouah, and murder all
the Christians who had taken refuge in that island.
The Turkish governor, Kalil Bey, fearful of not being
able to keep back the infuriated Turks, determined
at least to save the Europeans, and desired them to
take refuge in the ships which he placed at their disposal. The 5th of January, therefore, was spent in the
greatest confusion ; all our property had been removed
on board the vessels ; and, as my house was close to
the shore, the Europeans crowded into it, ready for
embarkation at a moment's notice.

"Towards evening, when every thing had been
prepared for our flight, I found myself alone with M.
de Jacobis. I then spoke to him more strongly than I
had ever done before ; telling him that it was entirely
owing to his obstinacy that I was incurring this great
danger ; and added, 'Through excess of humility,
you will not be made Bishop ; but in these missions
a Bishop is a victim, and not a spouse. Beware lest
self-love should be the cause of your resistance to
what I feel is the will of God.' Confounded at these
words, he threw himself at my feet, and told me to do
with him what I would. Fearing he might change
his mind, I instantly sent to beg the governor would
give me an escort of soldiers to guard my house for that
night, as I had some important business to transact

before I left. And so, having prepared every thing
for the service, I began the ceremony of consecration soon after midnight, assisted only by two of M.
de Jacobis' native priests; and by dawn the Office
was over.

" I had myself been consecrated at Rome, in the
church of St. Carlo, in the Corso, by the Cardinal
Franzoni, assisted by a multitude of other ecclesiastics,
Bishops and priests, and with a music and pomp which
ravished the crowd who took part in the ceremony.
At the consecration of M. de Jacobis, he and I were
alone; for the native priests, not understanding the
Latin rite, could only remain as passive statues; and,
instead of music, we only heard the menaces and roar-
ing of the infuriated mob without, who were clamour-
ing for our lives. But, nevertheless, the service was
so touching and so full of consolation, that we both
burst into tears. Here, indeed, was the victim prepared for the sacrifice—not the Bishop invested with
dignity and honour! Thus did he offer himself, like
our Divine Lord, as a living sacrifice for the people
of his adoption. He was Bishop for twelve years:
during that time he never wore the episcopal dress.
At the moment of consecration, to inaugurate him
in his new position, I was obliged to place my own
mitre on his head, my own ring on his finger, and to
give him my own crozier and pectoral cross. The
ceremony over, he resumed his poor tattered clothes,

and his Apostolic life of hardship and penury. Thus he lived, and thus he died, in the desert, under a little mimosa-tree (a specimen, by the by, of the *spina Christi*, meet emblem of the only crown he sought on earth); and thus did God send into Abyssinia this prodigy of humility, to be to them a living gospel, a true image of Him who was ' meek and humble of heart ;' one, in fact, who taught this benighted people, not by words, but by acts, what is the meaning of a real Catholic; so that multitudes might thus be led into the true fold, and that his converts, moved by the example of so great a model, might be filled with the same spirit, become worthy successors of the first *followers* of the Cross, and win, like them, the martyr's crown.''

CHAPTER VI.

Commencement of persecution—Visit of M. Poussou—Hardships of missionary life in Abyssinia.

THE consecration of Mgr. de Jacobis, and the arrival of Mgr. Massaja in his new diocese, had exasperated the heretical Bishop, the Abouna Salama, beyond all bounds. He resolved to organise a systematic persecution of the Catholics throughout the country; and the success of Mgr. de Jacobis' last mission at Gondar, under the powerful protection of the prince of that country, Ras-Aly, put the finishing stroke to his long-pent-up wrath and desire of vengeance.

The town of Gondar, once so famous in ancient Abyssinian history, is now but the shadow of the former great capital. It is situated in a fertile plain, at the foot of green hills covered with the richest vegetation. To judge by the ruins with which the plain is covered, the city must have been many miles in extent. Of all these ancient monuments, however, none remain standing but the imperial *château*, built by the Portuguese in 1680, when they came to defend the Abyssinian emperor against the Turks. It is a fortress flanked by four great towers. The rooms are almost all dismantled and uninhabitable; but such as are tolerably comfortable were at this time occupied by the phantom emperor, who still existed, and nominally reigned over the whole country. All his real power consisted in that of life and death over the inhabitants of Gondar itself. Although the kings who had supplanted him were obliged in public audiences to assume the position and title of slaves, yet, should the unhappy emperor happen to thwart their designs in any way, he was instantly suppressed, and one more accommodating put in his place. It is difficult to imagine what could be the object of keeping up this kind of fictitious imperialism, unless it were to flatter the national pride, and also that each petty king flattered himself that the day would come when this power might become a reality in his own individual case, as we shall presently see has actually happened. Ras-Aly, who was favourable to the missionaries, resided near Gondar, and granted them a site for a church and convent not only in the town itself, but also at Bietlhiem, a pretty *riant* country, in a good climate, and with an abundance of all kinds of provisions. Another mission-house and chapel were built in the district called Choho, schools were opened, and baptism was eagerly sought for by the people. But the Evil One could not see so rapid a progress without doing his best to impede it; and a persecution began, of which the following letter from Mgr. de Jacobis gives the first authentic details:

"Alitiena, December 13, 1853.

" The heretic clergy have worked up the government to proceed to active measures against the Church, and the first-fruits of this persecution has been the imprisonment of two of our native priests, and of a young girl named Woleta Berhan. She was of noble birth, but had relinquished all worldly advantages in order to embrace the religious state. Despising their tempting offers as much as their menaces, this beautiful child walked with a firm step in the midst of her hostile guards, with a face in which it was impossible to detect the least emotion of fear or anxiety. The people, however, moved at the sight, clamoured for her release, and that with such violence and excitement, that the satellites of the tyrant became alarmed for their own safety; and finally her chains were struck off, amidst the cheers of the mob, who accompanied her, in a kind of triumphal procession, back to her father's house. Let no religious order of women fear to come to this country: the Abyssinians have the greatest respect for Christ's spouses, and will defend them on every occasion at the risk of their own lives.

" The tyrant, foiled in this quarter, sent troops to seize us at Alitiena. I implored the students to seek safety in a more rapid flight, but they refused to leave me; so that, though my age impeded their movements, we managed, by the grace of God, to

reach a neighbouring forest, from whence a tortuous
path across the mountains conducted us, after seven
or eight hours' wearisome march, to a place of comparative safety. Here we held a council of war as
to our future movements; and finally we decided to
throw ourselves on the mercy of King Oubié, who,
though he had consented to this attack, was, I knew,
in heart disposed to befriend us. We arrived at the
camp in the night, but were treated as robbers, and
driven away with blows and menaces. Between the
alternative of being devoured by the hyenas outside,
or being massacred by the heretics within, I chose
the latter; and we deliberately seated ourselves close
to the door of the king's tent. Just at dawn, some
men approached us in silence, dressed in the long
"burnous," which serves both as cloak and bed to
the Abyssinians. They had spent the night in search-
ing for us; and on finding out where we were, they
joined us in prayer, beseeching our Lord to bless the
bold step we were about to take. One of these men
was a descendant of Licaonti, one of the most illustrious families of Ethiopia. He went to announce
our arrival to the king—a perilous office, recollecting
that we were exiled from the country by his orders.
To our great relief, the master of the ceremonies returned instantly with him, and conducted us to the
tents which Oubié had desired him to prepare for our
honourable reception. We, who had expected no-

thing but imprisonment and tortures, could scarcely believe our eyes and ears. All of a sudden, Tecla-Ghiorghis, one of our Abyssinian priests, exclaimed: ' On our knees! on our knees! Let us thank God!' The next day we appeared before our accusers, in presence of the king, whose manner convinced us at once that our persecution was against his will. It pleased God to confound the malice of our adversaries, who were unable to prove any of the charges which they had alleged against us; and so completely was the Abouna Salama convicted of perjury and untruth, that the whole audience cried shame upon him. The king then rose, and, after enumerating the benefits conferred by the Catholics upon the country, severely reproved his prime minister for having lent himself to the spiteful intrigues of the Abouna Salama, and ordered the instant release of all the Catholic prisoners. He wound up his speech with the following words: ' Let the Catholic priests teach, convert, and minister to my people as much as they will; the fewer Mahometans and pagans they leave in my country, the better I shall be pleased.'

" I had said nothing to Oubié of the unwarrantable attack made upon us at Alitiena, as our mission-house and church had been protected in an almost miraculous manner, and the officer in command of the expedition had been thrown from his horse and killed. This reserve on my part touched Cuocabié, who had

been the main instigator of this outrage; so that, out
of gratitude, he himself brought us back our imprisoned and now rescued brethren. It was a most
touching sight, and moved the hearts of all the people,
when the prisoners were brought out, loaded with
chains, while we kissed these mute witnesses of their
confessorship, and sang together joyful *Te Deums* to
Him who holds in His hand the hearts of kings. The
result of this outburst has been to strengthen our
hands and to weaken the position of the Coptic Bishop,
whom no one respects, although the terror of his ex-
communications on the one hand, and of his tortures
on the other, affects the progress which Catholicism
would otherwise make with unheard-of rapidity in
this country. I am sorry to say, that the English
policy has been in favour of the Abouna Salama,
whose character they do not know, having been mis-
led by the representations of a renegade Italian in
their service."

In the midst of these varied annoyances, intense
privations, and hair-breadth escapes,—of which Mgr.
de Jacobis himself speaks so lightly, that it is difficult
to realise the self-sacrifice and suffering which his
daily life entailed,—he had the consolation of a visit
from one of his own Congregation—M. Poussou,
assistant-superior—who was on his way back from
China, where he had been visiting the different missions
established in that country. The account of his visit

K

will enlighten us a little as to the nature of Mgr. de Jacobis' life.

"I arrived at Massouah," M. Poussou writes, " on the 9th of December, and found it to consist of a miserable collection of straw huts, which neither sheltered one from the overpowering heat of the sun nor from the torrents of rain which alternately try the endurance of Europeans in this country.

"Ten or twelve thousand people are congregated in this wretched island, living in the utmost misery, almost naked, and nearly all Mahometans. The thermometer never being lower than 80°, some idea may be formed of the burning nature of the climate; when I was there, the glass marked 85°.* From thence, I went to Emkoullou, which is in the middle of the Samahar desert, containing very few inhabitants, but full of hyenas, leopards, ostriches, gazelles, and, occasionally, lions. The Bedouins of this country are not very dark: they have fine figures and features, without the thick lips or wide nostril of the negroes, and enormous heads of hair, which they grease with butter or tallow, thus rendering them impervious to either sun or rain. At Emkoullou, Mgr. de Jacobis has purchased a house for the sisters of charity whom he hopes shortly to import there. I cannot say much for

---

* There is a native saying, that Pondicherry is the hottest place in India; but that Pondicherry is cool in comparison with Aden; and that Aden is cold compared with Massouah!

the building. It contains but four rooms, about ten
or twelve feet square, the whole covered by a flat roof
with a thin coating of lime; also, it affords no sort
of shelter against the rain. The evening of my arrival,
a sharp shower having come on, I found myself obliged
to sleep under my umbrella; and the next day it was
impossible to say Mass, the altar being drenched, like
every thing else. Hearing that Mgr. de Jacobis was at
Halaï, I resolved to follow him there; and started on
the 15th of December with M. Stella, he and I each
mounted on a mule, with five or six men to serve as
escort, armed—as is usual in Abyssinia—with lances,
cutlasses, and shields. Halaï is the first Abyssinian
village on the route to Adoua: it is situated on a
high plateau; and to get there, one must cross a very
high and precipitous mountain called Taranta. The
plain of Halaï is inhabited by about seven or eight
hundred peasants, who live by agriculture, and grow
oats, millet, lentils, and a little wheat. They pasture
their cattle in the mountains; working their fields
with oxen, which they use also as beasts of burden.
Until I undertook this journey, I had no conception
of what an Abyssinian missionary has to suffer. Without dwelling on the incredible heat and fatigues of the
journey, he has three things to fear: robbers, wild
beasts, and thorns. We had hardly set out, before an
enormous hyena started out of the bushes at the very
feet of my mule, and trotted off, making the most

awful cries. It is lucky that this carnivorous beast
is afraid of man, unless he can find him asleep; or
their horrible howl would be even more alarming.

" My fear of the wild beasts overcame all other sen-
sations, or the terrible thorns—which literally covered
the whole path, often barring our passage altogether,
and which pitilessly tore our clothes and skin—
would have made the march sufficiently disagreeable.
By night I was so utterly exhausted, that I could do
literally nothing; while M. Stella, more accustomed
to these wearisome journeys, busied himself in getting
our supper. In Abyssinia, a traveller does not take
bread with him, but flour. This flour they mix with
a little water; put it on to boil; and then throw it
into a frying-pan for a few minutes, when it comes
out in the shape of a flat, thin cake, which one eats
hot. Sometimes, to make it crisper, they roll the
flour round a stone, and put it on the charcoal for
a few moments. But the flour is so bad, that, at
best, this food is very uneatable; and, to grind the
flour itself, one has only a couple of round stones, the
grit of which mingles with the bread.

" The next day, to avoid the tremendous thorns,
we turned into a mountain-gorge, crossing a stream
which a day's rain converts into so formidable a
torrent, that whole caravans have been swept away
by it. This gorge is very narrow, but extremely
beautiful, with magnificent trees and flowers; the

rocks on either side assuming the grandest and most fantastic shapes. It can only be traversed in safety by day, as it is to these streams that the lions come down to drink at night. A multitude of birds, gazelles, antelopes, monkeys, marmots, and other smaller animals, crossed our path in every direction; and the grateful shade compensated for some of the intense suffering of the previous day.

"That evening, however, we arrived at the foot of the mountain; and here our real fatigues began. The ascent was so precipitous, that the mules became useless; we could only scramble up by our hands and feet. The track leads over awful precipices; and the stones are so slippery, that it was with the utmost difficulty, and after many bad tumbles, that I could keep my feet at all. The ascent lasted for four hours. Towards the summit, the temperature became infinitely cooler, and little patches of hoar-frost even appeared here and there in the hollows. I was, however, so completely exhausted, that I had hardly strength to mount my mule, and descend the mountain to the village below. To my great disappointment, on arriving at Halaï, I found that Mgr. de Jacobis would not be back there for two days. But the good Brother Filippini did his best to make me comfortable in their new mission. The house passes for a mansion in this country, being built of earth, which is considered a great luxury; but it has neither window

nor chimney; and one is suffocated by the smoke of
the kitchen-fire, which almost excludes the little light
given by the open door. This primitive episcopal
palace had a little courtyard, surrounded with a thorn
or euphorbia hedge to keep out the hyenas; and the
only entrance was closed by a huge fagot of thorns,
lowered at night, and raised like a portcullis by day.
The only decent corner of the house had been converted into a little chapel, where daily Mass was said.
Our Lord must, indeed, have found Himself in a
poorer cave even than Bethlehem upon that Christ-
mas night! To make our altar-breads, we were compelled to take the bottoms of a little tin case, and run
some flour between them. Such were our Christmas-
day Masses!

"At a little distance from the village, there is a
cool valley, with a stream running through it, shaded
by some fine trees. There, while waiting for my good
Bishop, I used to spend most of my time, thereby
escaping the intense heat, as also the darkness and
smoke, of the house. At first, the peasants left me
in peace; but I having unwisely given them some
medals and pictures, their importunity left me no
further rest or chance of quiet. On the fourth day,
however, to my intense joy, Mgr. de Jacobis arrived.
It is difficult for me to describe the effect he produced
upon me. A man so holy, so humble, so mortified,
so charitable, so patient, and, withal, so gay and

cheerful, I have never seen before or since. Living
in the midst of the greatest privations, behaving himself as the lowest of all, with no clothes but a coarse
shirt and drawers, and a bit of linen round his head,
sleeping on a cow's skin, and eating food which, to a
European, is next to impossible, he has so completely
crucified his human nature, that the hardships of his
position never seem to occur to him. He is looked
upon by the whole country as a saint; and this impression is made upon every one with whom he comes
in contact. No sooner had he arrived, than the little
community fell into its regular habits. Every one
met in the chapel at dawn; but he was always there
before us. He proposed the subject of the day's
meditation, gave a little outline of the principal points,
and always ended with some practical reflection bearing on the occupations of the day. Very often he
gave an abridged history of the saint of the day, with
a few words of application to ourselves. After this
came the *Angelus* and the Litany of the Name of
Jesus; and then he celebrated the Holy Sacrifice.
This over, we all went into the kitchen, and drank
a cup of coffee without sugar; he exchanging a few
kind and cheering words with each. From the kitchen
we passed into the community-room. There every
one took his Breviary and said Office, Mgr. de Jacobis
making them recite the Psalms in the Gheez dialect,
—by which means the Psalter was gone through in

fifteen days. Then he fixed the occupations of each
for the day—instruction of children, study of native
dialects, and the like. If any had a doubt or difficulty, he would take this opportunity of courting an
explanation or a solution. On all Fridays, they had
the Way of the Cross. On Sundays and feast-days,
he preached on the Gospel for the day, and catechised.
He strongly inculcated frequent communion. Towards evening, they made time for spiritual reading
in community, ending with a portion of the Bible,
and some practical reflections on the lives of the
saints. At sunset, they all recited the Rosary together—from which devotion he was never absent;
and then they sang the *Salve Regina* and the *Ave
Maria*. All his priests and students were treated
alike—he allowed no preferences or distinctions. In
the same way, he was severe against any breach of
charity amongst them. If one of them had done
wrong, he would take upon himself the penance or
mortification the fault had entailed, in spite of the
tears and entreaties of the offender. He had but one
dress, and, when it wanted washing, he was compelled
to borrow one from the others during the operation.
On the vigils of the great feasts, he slept at the foot
of the altar. On those days, his Mass lasted sometimes an hour and a half, or two hours, from the
consecration to the end. We all watched him with
awe : his face was, as it were, transfigured ; his whole

body trembled; and it seemed as if the Spirit of God were visibly present within him. There is no doubt that he has been raised up by God for the conversion of this people, among whom his influence is perfectly extraordinary. An old man—the father of the governor of Halaï—used to come every morning to learn his catechism from Mgr. de Jacobis, like a little child. God employed extraordinary means to effect his conversion; and, soon after, he was attacked by an illness which threatened fatal results. He instantly sent for Mgr. de Jacobis, and implored him to give him the Sacraments of the Church. He made his general confession with such expressions of hope, faith, charity, and contrition, that the good Bishop was touched to tears; and he then received the last Sacraments with a fervour and joy which astonished the assistants. Presently he heard the usual Abyssinian wail echoing through the streets; for he was much beloved and respected by his tribe. 'Who is it who is weeping thus?' he exclaimed, reopening his dying eyes. 'My friends—my children—why these cries and tears? Do you not know that I am going to Him who has redeemed me with His Blood? Rejoice rather in my consolation, and sing praises to God.' And thus this good old man slept in our Lord.

"His last request had been, that no priest but Mgr. de Jacobis and his missionaries should attend his funeral, or perform any portion of the service. The

Coptic clergy had, however, assembled in great numbers; and Mgr. de Jacobis, unwilling to be the cause
of contention at such a moment, yielded his office to
them. They, touched by his humility, not only begged
him to perform the funeral rites, but openly declared
themselves willing to abjure their heretical opinions
and follow the 'Abouna Jacob,' as they called him.
Vested, therefore, according to the gorgeous Ethiopian
rite, preceded by a magnificent cross, with acolytes
swinging censers, and an immense procession, Mgr.
de Jacobis was able, for the first time, to celebrate an
office of the Church in a befitting manner. The effect
on the people was immense. The clergy of the neighbourhood all placed their churches and schools at his
disposal, and implored Mgr. de Jacobis to baptise and
instruct their children.

"Two or three days' journey from the mission-
house, and not far from Kaïguor—the battle-field of
the Ethiopians against the Moors, so vaunted by their
poets—there is a very curious tract of country, forming, as it were, a deep basin hemmed round by arid
mountains. A fresh stream runs through the valley,
and a large pastoral population is scattered among
the trees, forming six separate villages. This district,
which bears the name of Zana-Daglié, sent for Mgr. de
Jacobis, and, having sworn fidelity to him as to their
spiritual head, implored him to baptise their children.
They brought thirty the first day, and forty the next.

Their second petition was, that he should lay the
foundation-stone of two new churches, which they
had made a subscription among themselves to build.
This he did, to the intense joy of the people, especially
of the venerable old ' King of the Sea,' as one of these
petty princes was called. This old chieftain asked but
for one thing, and that was for a picture of the Virgin
and Child which had been exposed that day under a
pretty green canopy, and which had excited his
greatest admiration. A large cross had been placed
in the centre of each village, and it was most touching to see these poor people, on returning from their
work, kneel with the greatest devotion at the foot of
this emblem of our salvation, and repeat in their own
dialect the usual Catholic prayers, which Mgr. de
Jacobis had translated for them.

"But my duties called me elsewhere; and with
great sorrow I parted with Abyssinia's great apostle,
and retraced my steps towards the Red Sea. The more
I saw of Mgr. de Jacobis' life and labours, the more
I perceived the hand of God in his appointment—the
very persecutions which he was enduring only serving
to spread the knowledge of the Cross into fresh districts, and enabling him to sow the seed of truth
broadcast over this great country, for which he was
so soon about to give his life."

CHAPTER VII.

Early history of Cassa, the future Emperor Theodoros—Consecration of Mgr. Biancheri, and of the new church at Evo.

WHILST in the east Mgr. de Jacobis was daily conquering souls for Christ, in the west a common soldier was making rapid strides towards supreme power, had overthrown Ras-Aly, and threatened to seize the whole empire of Abyssinia—in which enterprise he finally succeeded. As the history of this man has become, in consequence of recent political events, very interesting to Englishmen at the present moment, we will give his biography in full.

Cassa, now styled the Emperor Theodoros, and the most successful adventurer that this century has, perhaps, ever known, was born in the province of Quarata. His father was a humble peasant, and his mother was a simple dealer in *cusso*, the vermifuge of Abyssinia, which is now so generally used in European medicine. Cassa is between thirty and thirty-five years of age, tall and well-made, with an air of great dignity, and a certain consciousness of power which belongs to those destined to take the lead in human affairs. In 1850, he enlisted as a common soldier in the army of Ras-Aly, Prince of Gallas, and the most powerful of

Abyssinia's petty kings. By his good looks, his in-sinuating manners, and the promise which he gave of future distinction, he obtained the hand of a natural daughter of the king's in marriage. But soon after, piqued at the conduct of the royal family towards him, whom they looked upon as a *parvenu*, Cassa suddenly deserted his master's camp, and, with a few devoted followers, set up the standard of revolt.

Waldirad, general of Ras-Aly's forces, gave notice of Cassa's proceedings to his master, adding, "Sire, I will start instantly in pursuit of this insolent brigand; by to-morrow night the son of the peasant dealer in *cusso* shall be dragged in humble submission to your feet." Accordingly, Waldirad, with an army of 4000 men, bore down the next day upon Cassa, who, with a handful of tried veterans, awaited his attack in the plain of Ciacio. At the very first onslaught, Waldirad fell into the enemy's hands; and, to add to his humiliation, the conqueror, presenting him with a bowl of *cusso*, said in his ear, "Eat, my friend, some of the *cusse* of my good mother. You can have it cheap." This victory attracted others to Cassa's standard. With 300 men, he marched against Ras-Aly himself at Dagussa, defeated him, and dictated on the ground conditions of peace.

But with this world's heroes, as with Christians, it is in the school of suffering and reverses that characters are formed. Cassa, flushed with success, strove to

acquire fresh laurels in the west of Abyssinia. He
attacked the Egyptians, who were encamped on the
route to Sennaar, in the mountains of Matamma,
having the tribe of Bal-Acomada (or sack-bearers) as
auxiliaries. But the Egyptians were well prepared, and
they opened such a fire of artillery upon their aggres-
sors that an ignominious flight was the result. Cassa
speedily discovered that the principal cause of his
defeat was a relative of his own, who, having been
brought up from his childhood in Egypt, had there
learnt the art of war, and was now acting as pacha and
commander of the fort. He understood at once the
advantage of disciplined troops against a levy of raw
recruits, and resolved to win this pacha over to his
side. The skill and address which he showed in these
negotiations gave evidence of great powers of government; and, having won the confidence and esteem of
his *ci-devant* enemy, he determined at once to initiate
his band into the new methods of warfare which gave
the Egyptians so marked a superiority over the Abyssinians. The first thing was to obtain the necessary
firearms, and Cassa stuck at nothing to accomplish his
ends. He even robbed all passing travellers, especially
such as possessed rifles. The French traveller, M.
Rochet d'Héricourt, being at Gondar, was reported to
Cassa as possessing arms of that description; an instant summons to give them up was the result. The
Frenchman refused, and was consequently thrown

into a dungeon and heavily chained. Then Cassa
became alarmed at the political consequences of his
act, and released him in person, with the usual
Abyssinian apology of *"Maregna, ghietaie, maregna"*
—" Pardon, sir, pardon"—bearing, at the same time,
on his shoulder, a large stone in token of penitence,
according to the custom of his people. Cassa was,
however, still in the position of an outlaw, when an
event happened which altogether changed the state of
affairs.

We have before spoken of the intense veneration
felt throughout Abyssinia for the imperial dynasty,
and the universal belief in its descent from Solomon
himself; so that, though the possessor of the illustrious and hereditary title was virtually a prisoner,
still none else dared arrogate the title of " emperor"
to himself; and Oubié and Ras-Aly had contented
themselves with the simpler appellations of viceroy and
general-in-chief. The mother of Ras-Aly, however, an
ambitious and intriguing woman, greatly coveted the
title of empress, which could only be obtained by
her union with a prince of the real blood-royal. *Ce
que femme veut, Dieu veut,* runs the proverb ; and so,
after many obstacles, the lady's wish was accomplished
—she was married, and proclaimed at once *Ittièque,*
or empress. With the imperial crown on her brow,
and a determination in her heart that her reign should
be illustrious, she organised her son's forces, and

advanced at the head of a numerous army into the plain of Dagussa, with the openly expressed determination of annihilating the "brigand Cassa," as she termed him, and driving him from the face of the earth. The two hostile camps were ranged in battle array, only divided by a narrow strip of volcanic land, which the tropical rains had converted into a quagmire of liquid mud. But what obstacle could stand in the way of the new empress? "Forward, men of Gallas!" she exclaimed; "forward!—exterminate these rebels!" No one stirred. "Poltroons, cowards," she continued, "you are afraid! Well, I, a woman, will fight alone. The daughter of the leopard has no need of you." She sprang on her mule, who leapt across the sea of liquid mud towards the hostile camp, the Gallas troops looking on, speechless and curious. What could an unfortunate woman do, unaided, against an army? Already she was in the enemy's power. Cassa was quietly waiting for her on the opposite bank; and, on turning round to see if her unworthy troops had been moved by her brave example, and were about to come to the rescue, she perceived, on the contrary, that they were busily engaged in pillaging her tent, and were about to take to flight with their inglorious booty. Cassa, to do him justice, proved himself a generous enemy. He treated the fallen princess with great honour, and accepted, in exchange for his illustrious prisoner,

certain lands belonging to Ras-Aly, who gladly thus
obtained his mother's release. These lands, however,
adjoined the territory of Goschou—or the "Buffalo"
—one of Abyssinia's most valiant commanders. The
truce with Ras-Aly having been soon broken, the
"Buffalo" met Cassa in the plain of Dembra. Victory seemed on the point of declaring itself in
Goschou's favour, when a ball pierced him in the
forehead. He fell down dead, and his army instantly
took to flight. Rifled arms being new to the Abyssinians,—and Cassa, with the assistance of his young
Egyptian relative, having trained his troops in the use
of these weapons,—no native army had a chance of
success. Seven years ago, M. d'Abbadié, hearing of
Cassa, had told Goschou, "Mark my words, this
young fellow, of whom you think so little, will one
day be master of all Abyssinia."

At the news of the astounding success of Cassa,
all Abyssinia took fright. Oubié and Ras-Aly, for-
getting their former feuds, resolved to combine against
the common enemy. Oubié sent his two best generals, Walda Ghiorghis and Aloula, with five strong
detachments of infantry. Ras-Aly's troops, which
were still more numerous, with a large body of
well-mounted cavalry, joined them in the plains of
Gorgora, a site famous in the annals of Christian
missions, and which was destined to witness another
important battle. Cassa, who had been brought up

L

by Ras-Aly's general as a son, behaved towards him
with the dutiful love of a child. "For God's sake,
my father," he exclaimed, " do not persist in this un-
equal contest; withdraw your forces while there is yet
time. Do not burden me with the sin of a parricide."
But Ras-Aly's commander-in-chief knew too well his
duty as a soldier to be shaken by Cassa's representations. He gave the signal for battle, and the two
armies were speedily engaged in a hand-to-hand strife,
in which Cassa was completely victorious, and his friend,
as he had foreseen, fell almost immediately, riddled with
balls. Thus ended this fatal struggle. The conqueror
buried the hostile general with almost royal honours,
thereby to testify both his affection and his sorrow. His
son, who had retired into the fastnesses of Amba Semma,
that famous mountain of Godjam,—which Nature has
made completely impregnable,—burning with desire to
avenge his father's death, moved heaven and earth to
bring together fresh troops against Cassa, but without
result. Cassa then sent him a message to this effect :
" Thy father is dead, but he has died the death of
a hero. Make peace with me, and together we will
fight against the common enemy, and reëstablish the
Abyssinian empire as in the ancient days." Berrou-
Goschou yielded to these flattering words, and, coming
down from his fortress, joined Cassa's troops in the
plain. From that hour, every thing was lost for
Abyssinia's petty kings. On the 15th June, the two

great armies met once more in deadly combat. But
the star of Cassa was ever in the ascendant. The
troops of Ras-Aly, seized with a sudden panic, threw
down their arms and fled. Ras-Aly in vain endeavoured, by prodigies of valour, to retrieve the
fortunes of the day. With his own hand he cut down
seven noted warriors, including the famous Mussulman
chief Daganièro; and at the last, finding the game
hopeless, he cut his way through masses of the enemy,
and went to take refuge in the inaccessible mountains of "the Werro-Gallas." A Scotchman, named
John Bell, remained faithful to his master during that
terrible day, and fought like a lion by his side. Cassa,
on the other hand, had a henchman equally devoted
to his service in the person of Dominico, a man of
half-Italian, half-Greek origin, who alone was able
to cope with Caledonia's son; and each performed
prodigies of valour in the defence of their respective
masters on that eventful day.

But Cassa was not satisfied with temporal dominion; he aspired likewise to be the spiritual head
of his people. This "Nicolas with a Small Foot," as
the Abyssinians called him, began by sending an im-
perative message to the Abouna Salama, commanding
him to join his camp. Cassa had hitherto protected
the Catholic Christians established at Gondar and elsewhere, and had sent courteous messages to Mgr. de
Jacobis, assuring him of his assistance and protection.

But from the moment that he was crowned Emperor, he adopted a new line of policy : making use of the Abouna Salama to persecute the Church on the one hand ; but, on the other, being equally hostile to the Abouna's own sect, and to the Protestant missionaries sent from time to time into his country. Apostolical zeal, of whatever sort, found in him a most bitter and implacable enemy ; and the ambitious adventurer had no longer any aim but one : *the union of Church and State under one head—that head to be himself.*

But to return to Mgr. de Jacobis. In the midst of the tumult of civil war, his missions went on ever increasing ; more churches were built, fresh schools were opened ; and his neophytes prepared themselves, by daily combats and sufferings, for the persecution which he foresaw would soon come upon the Church. For persecution was certain, especially after the union between the new Emperor Theodoros and the Abouna Salama, that half Mussulman, half Eutychian prelate, to whom the success of Mgr. de Jacobis had from the first been as gall and wormwood. Before speaking of this time of trial, we will say a few words of the consolations which our holy Bishop was permitted to receive during this interval of comparative tranquillity, the last before the final outbreak which was to end in his martyrdom and death.

In January 1854, he writes : " In the midst of wars and rumours of wars, you may be interested in

knowing how we are getting on in our large harvest-
field, which—thank God!—is every day extending.
Whole populations have lately come to us, offering to
restore their ruined churches, and imploring us to
baptise their children, to open schools, and to give
them books in their own languages, which are always
eagerly read.

"A large number of native priests have been
established in these new districts, who, by their zeal
and devotion, greatly contribute to raise the estimate
of the Catholic faith in the minds of the people. We
had just returned from a visitation of these new missions, when M. Biancheri arrived, who, to my great
joy, had at last consented to receive episcopal consecration, and become my coadjutor in this vast country.
The ceremony took place in our poor little chapel of
Halaï, on the day of the feast of the Rosary. The
episcopal cross was only of wood, ingeniously carved
by our good Brother Filippini; the mitre and sandals
were the work of M. Biancheri himself; Dom Zacharia
Cahen lent us a pair of coarse gray woollen gloves;
and one single pectoral cross and one poor ring served
for the consecrator and the consecrated. For assistant-
Bishops, we had but two native priests. Yet a great
joy and a great peace fell upon the performers of this
ceremony, so brilliant in evangelical poverty; and no
sooner was it over, than the newly elected prelate started
off to the scene of his future labours, i. e. the vast mis-

sion of M. Stella : whilst I, thanking God for such an
auxiliary against the wolves who ravaged my flock,
set off to visit the kingdoms of Gondar and Choa.

"On my way I was to consecrate the new church
at Evo. These people had degenerated into a species
of Theism, and had lost even the recollection of what
a church was. When I arrived, the whole population
was hurrying to a wood which, from time immemorial,
has been dedicated to the Blessed Virgin, there to implore her intercession for rain, which was much wanted.

"'What are you doing?' I exclaimed. 'Why
do you come here, instead of going to the church?'
'Because it is not consecrated,' they replied, 'and
the bulls are not yet killed for the feast.' This
reply was conclusive. 'Fix a day,' I answered, 'and
the consecration shall take place.' '*Felseta, Felseta!*'
they cried (' the day of the Assumption'). So I instantly sent to Massouah for an old bell—which an
unlucky crack had rendered certainly the reverse of
harmonious, and which, for want of a clapper, required to be vigorously struck from the outside—but
still a bell; which arrived triumphantly on the shoulders
of four stout peasants, who made their entry into the
town in the midst of the rejoicings of the inhabitants,
whose admiration knew no bounds. Unheard of,
besides, was the splendour of our consecration. The
pavement of the church was covered with a mat of
palm-leaves, on which were laid two Persian and

Turkish rugs; a beautiful candelabrum, the gift of our
good sisters at Paris, hung in the nave; and on
either side were pictures of our Lord and of His
Mother,—pious offerings from M. Torti of Rome, and
from the Princess Pignatelli at Naples. I really think
our good parishioners thought themselves already at
the gates of paradise.

"In Abyssinia, the whole ceremony of the consecration of a church consists in placing what they call
the *tabot*, or altar. This altar, sometimes in wood,
sometimes in stone, is made in the shape of a square,
or parallelogram. It is generally constructed of a
polished kind of agate called *Ebn-Bered*, but sometimes of *wonza*—a very hard wood, as incorruptible
as the cedar. This tree has a flower of which the
perfume is so delicious, that when the month of
October comes, which is the season for its flowering,
the whole tree is covered with bees to such an extent
as to give it the appearance of a huge hive. They
have a curious custom of hiding the *tabot*, or altar-
stone, the night before the consecration, and then
suddenly discovering it; perhaps in allusion to the
sacred fire hid by Jeremiah, and miraculously
recovered at the consecration of the second temple.
According to this tradition, soon after my arrival at
Evo, and on the eve of the ceremony, the priest went
with the *tabot* into the deepest recesses of the wood;
and the next morning, at dawn, the noise of trumpets,

mingled with that of the poor cracked bell, summoned
the whole population of the five surrounding villages
to the principal square ; when a troop of young men,
armed with spears and bucklers, started off to hunt
through the woods for the priest and the altar-stone.
The one who makes the discovery first, offers a bull
in sacrifice, and is considered the hero of the feast.
No sooner had he found the object of their search, than
he burst out singing a warlike and patriotic song
with a stentorian voice, which was taken up by all
the rest, who rushed forward to meet him. They
made a circle round the priest, singing and dancing ;
while the precious *tabot*, wrapped in a piece of fine
silk or other costly stuff, was borne triumphantly on
their heads to the newly erected church. This joyous
procession was met at the entrance of the village by
the young shepherdesses, whose sweeter voices mingled not unpleasantly with the rest; then came the
Defteras, or doctors, chanting Psalms in Gheez and
other dialects, clapping their hands, and beating their
iron-pointed staves on the ground; and then the
priests, with their acolytes swinging censers; the cross
being carried before the Bishop, all vested in sacer-
dotal garments. The whole ceremony, with the noise
of the trumpets and the enthusiasm of the *people*,
reminded one of the description, in Holy Writ, of the
transportation of the holy Ark to Mount Sion. After
this, a kind of tournament followed, carried on with

great skill and agility on either side, and resembling the ancient gladiatorial exhibitions of Rome and Greece. I waited rather impatiently, I must own, at the door of the church, with all my clergy, for the termination of this exhibition; feeling, however, that it would have been unwise to prohibit a national custom, harmless in itself, and to which the people attached so much importance. The tournament over, the whole assembly walked in procession three times round the church, repeating the Consecration Psalms; and then I celebrated the Holy Sacrifice. Every man, woman, and child took part in the service with the greatest earnestness and devotion, and a very large number received the Holy Communion from their Bishop's hand. A solemn Benediction closed the day's services, of which the remembrance will ever remain in my heart—as, I feel sure, it will in theirs. The result was not only an evanescent enthusiasm, but a solid conversion of a great many to the faith of Christ, of the reality of which we had abundant proofs when the days of fiery trial came.

"But our enemies did not leave us long in peace. The emissaries of the Abouna Salama first excited the Mussulmans to rob our church (although our sacred vessels were eventually restored); and then summoned a council of *Defteras* and Coptic monks to accuse us of having usurped their sanctuaries and seduced their flock, although they had been quite

content hitherto to leave both in ruins and utter ne-
glect. A conference was proposed; and when the
day came, one of our students spoke with such ability and good sense, that our opponents were utterly
confounded, and confusion was sown in the hostile
camp. I profited by the opportunity to read aloud,
with a firm voice, the following passage from the
Fethé-Neghest, or civil and religious code of Abyssinia,
which contains this most curious profession of faith :

" ' In the same way that the father has authority
and jurisdiction over his sons, the Bishop over his
subjects, and the Patriarch over the suffragan Bishops,
so, in the like manner, the Patriarch of Rome, in his
quality of successor to St. Peter, Prince of the Apostles, has authority and sovereign jurisdiction over all
the Patriarchs in the universal Church, and over all
human society,—holding, as he does, the place of
Jesus Christ, and being His Vicar upon earth.'

" These astounding words from their own sacred
books produced the most magical effect. Not only
was every hostile mouth stopped, but a large part
of the audience burst out laughing, and loudly
declared their adherence to the Catholic faith. The
enraged Copts proceeded to hide their defeat by
violent personal abuse; and finally pronounced a sentence of excommunication not only against all of us,
but against all those who had joined our Communion.
Then three of the Elders rose, and, with great wrath

and yet dignity, exclaimed : ' Impostors ! not content
with answering grave arguments by personal invec-
tives, you pretend to ignore the words of our sacred
books. Read them, and the veriest child can see that
the Catholics alone have the truth on their side.
Retract your words; or beware lest the excommunica-
tions you have so rashly pronounced should fall upon
yourselves.' The terrified priests, fearful of some
outburst of popular fury, accepted these humiliating
conditions, and humbly asked our pardon : after
which, the assembly dispersed ; but only to carry into
their distant villages the news of our triumph, and
the discomfiture of the enemies of the Church."

CHAPTER VIII.

Persecution and imprisonment of Mgr. de Jacobis and his flock—
Martyrdom of Abba Ghebra Mikael.

THE lull we have related in the preceding pages was
as if to prepare and strengthen our holy Bishop and
his valiant confessors for greater and more serious
storms. Driven from Guala, Alitiena, and Halaï, by
a succession of persecutions, Mgr. de Jacobis in 1853
found himself compelled to take refuge in the little
house of Emkoullou, near Massouah. But he, burning with desire for martyrdom, would not be content
to remain quiet till the fury of the adversary was
past. Under the pretext of making his usual visitation of the Christians in Choa and Godjam, he
started on foot, in spite of his age (for he was now
fifty-four, and broken by fatigues and hardships),
and arrived at Gondar, which was the head-quarters
of his great enemy, the Abouna Salama. He at once
wrote to Cassa, who had just been crowned Emperor, to ask for a safe conduct, and for permission to
remain as long as he wished in that capital. Cassa
replied : " Remain until the Abouna Salama arrives ;
and then we will have a public discussion, and see
which of you two has the truth on his side."

This, however, did not at all suit Salama, who wrote to say that he would not return to Gondar as long as Mgr. de Jacobis was allowed to remain there; at the same time threatening Cassa with all the terrors of the Church, if he did not at once drive out of the place this " insolent innovator." Cassa, alarmed less at the terrors of the Church than at the political mischief which might be the result of the Abouna Salama's openly taking part against him, desired Mgr. de Jacobis to leave Gondar. The latter protested that he had no right to abandon his post without the consent and knowledge of the Pope. Then Cassa gave him and his missionaries up to the tender mercies of the Abouna Salama. They were all seized by his orders, and separated—Mgr. de Jacobis under the care of the governor, the rest in different prisons. Salama desired that the Bishop should be sent to the desert of Sennaar; but the rainy season, which had set in, made the journey impossible. So he lingered on in a horrible dungeon for three months, and during that time wrote the following letter to his Superior-General at Paris :

" From my Prison at Gondar,
" July 1854.

" It is difficult for me to write to you freely from hence, as I do not know whether my letters will or will not be intercepted ; but I am anxious to let you

know the details of our present position, and the circumstances which have unexpectedly led to it.

" No sooner had Cassa established his authority
by force of arms, than he prepared to consolidate it
by several wise and pacific measures, especially by
the abolition of slavery, the prohibition of the muti-
lation of the bodies of men slain in battle, and a
careful revision of the laws. Having defeated Ras-
Aly and captured King Oubié, he forced the latter
to witness his own coronation as Emperor ; and thus
reëstablished in his own person the empire of Abyssinia, which had been virtually in abeyance since the
death of Tecla-Ghiorghis at Axuma, thirty-eight years
ago. But his ambition was not yet satisfied.

" Abyssinia was rent with internal divisions, of
which religion was the main cause. The new Emperor began by preaching a crusade against Islam-
ism, which he banished from his territories ; his kingdom now extending from Massouah in the east to
Khartoun in the west, and including the country of
the Gallas and other tribes to the south. But the
divisions among his Christian subjects gave him
more serious anxiety ; and, determining to unite them
all in one profession of faith under one head, he
called into his counsels the crafty Abouna Salama ;
and, by making him his tool, resolved to climb to
supreme ecclesiastical power, as he had previously
done to the civil. This union with Salama was the

signal for our destruction. No sooner had he arrived,
than Cassa called a council and addressed them as
follows : ' Know that I am the new Constantine, of
the great empire of Abyssinia, the elect of God, sent
to bring you back to the ways of unity and peace.'
These words were followed by an all-important act :
the drawing up, under the direction of Salama, of a
new Confession of Faith, to be believed in and sworn to
by all the people. This new *Credo* horrified not only
our faithful band of Catholics, but the most important and best-educated of the sectarians—the *Zaga-
leg*, as they are called—who sent a strong deputation
and remonstrance to Abouna Salama, asking for an
explanation, and declaring the new formula to be
pure Eutychianism, and condemned by all their sacred
books. Then the Abouna showed himself in his true
colours, and, with unparallelled audacity, proclaimed
this new gospel as the ' only truth' to his astonished
auditors. Cries of ' Heresy ! heretic !' interrupted
his oration. The Abouna, furious at this unexpected
resistance, fulminated imprecations and excommuni-
cations right and left. The *Zaga-leg*, as a last resource, appealed to Cassa—a fatal delusion, only too
soon to be dispelled ! He vouchsafed no answer to
their petition ; but one day arrived unexpectedly at
his palace, went into the gallery—which is a kind
of raised tribune overlooking the principal square—
summoned the whole town to attend, and then and

there, in presence of the people, caused the new edict
to be read; after which the Abouna, with an assur-
ance worthy of a better cause, solemnly declared,
in the face of heaven and earth, that the words they
had just heard were those of truth, and the only
doctrine of the Bible; that he was ready to seal this
oath with his blood; and that it behoved all men
calling themselves Christians to follow his example.
He had scarcely done speaking, when Cassa, pistol
in hand, came forward and threatened with tortures,
imprisonment, or death, whoever differed from the
'saint-like and incomparable Bishop Salama.' Then
came the melancholy spectacle of the apostasy of hundreds of souls, whom terror had kept mute during
this terrible and unexpected scene. Cassa, with a
proud and self-satisfied face, received the oaths of his
perjured people; and, to crown the deplorable per-
formance, the formula of excommunication (or inter-
diction from fire and water) was pronounced against
the unfortunate and inoffensive nominal emperor,
Azié-Johannès, who had dared to resist the imperial
decree. And thus ended a day so memorable in the
religious annals of Abyssinia.

"And now what remains, in the face of error so
gigantic, and a power so relentlessly exercised ? Nothing but Catholicism—now, as ever, poor, humble,
the scorn of the earth; but constant, faithful, universally recognised and triumphant, even in the

midst of suffering and death. A glorious contrast
was presented by our people that day to the otherwise universal spectacle of weak compliance with the
Emperor's decree on the part of the different Abyssinian sects.

"During many previous months, I had not ceased
to warn my Catholic children of the impending danger,
and to implore them to seek safety in flight. They
invariably refused, saying ' they would not leave me ;
and that, if the hour were at hand when they would have
to confess their faith before men, they should rejoice in
suffering for our Lord, and in thus bearing witness,
however feebly, to the truth.' Summoned, in consequence, to repeat the new *Credo* in common with
the rest, their only answer was a triple confession
of their belief in the one holy Catholic and Roman
faith ; to the great exaltation of.their mother Church,
and the rage and confusion of our enemies. Their
confession was instantly followed by imprisonment
in a loathsome dungeon, and the torture of the *ghend*,
from which they have never been released for the last
two months. This terrible punishment, like one of
the same sort among the Chinese, consists in a large
piece of the heaviest kind of wood, with an oval
opening sufficiently wide to admit the legs of the
prisoner, which are tightly pressed together, and then
fastened with a heavy chain, which, passing with
difficulty between the legs, fixes them as in a vice ;

M

so that, to release them, it is necessary to saw the wood asunder. The wretched sufferer must either remain constantly sitting, or with the dismal alternative of lying on his back on the damp floor of a dungeon which is reeking with filth and abominable insects. Among these confessors are: Abba Ghebra Mikael, sixty-six years old; a man of high birth, eminent for science, and an admirable poet. He was one of the original deputation to Rome, and the first on whom I had conferred priest's orders. He had suffered imprisonment before for his faith, being incarcerated for three months in 1849. But this time he was so severely beaten, when first seized, that he was left for dead. Abba Tecla-Immanot, also a priest, with his father, mother, brother, and younger sister (who is a nun), have all been imprisoned and tortured, beaten on the face, and confined in the terrible *ghend.* Abba Tesfa Zion, Abba Tecla-Michael, and other monks, although not priests, have been subjected to the like punishments. Their little notes to me, which I receive from time to time, are indeed a consolation in the midst of the sorrow I cannot help feeling, humanly speaking, for their great physical sufferings, which are aggravated by the intense heat. I give you one or two specimens:

" ' Welcome to our dear spiritual father and friend ! Thanks to the Divine goodness, all goes well with us. Now, at last, we are allowed to drink

of our Master's cup, of which we had feared to be
found unworthy. Pray for us, that our faith and
courage may not fail. We are in want of nothing,
except your prayers. When trials come upon us
against our will, we suffer, and are grieved ; but
when one seeks for suffering, and embraces it with
joy, how can one feel sorrow ?'

" Again :

" ' To our dear venerable father and Bishop, from
his children, who have remained faithful and constant
to his teaching ; not through their own strength, but
by the grace of our Divine Lord and of His immacu-
late Mother. Many grateful thanks for what you have
sent us, which we look upon as a gift from our saint
of to-day (St. A. Liguori), our much-loved patron.'
(I had sent them some honey.) ' How wonderful are
the ways of the Divine wisdom ! From the salt and
bitter ocean arise the mists which irrigate our land ;
and. so, from the depths of our dark dungeon, our
holy faith shines brighter than ever it did before.
Seated night and day on a damp stone, with our
feet in the terrible *ghend*, we preach without moving.
Our tongues may be mute, but our tortured limbs
proclaim aloud, " Believe in the one holy Catholic
Church." Ah ! pray for us, dearest father ; pray
earnestly that we may have constancy unto the end.
We feel terribly for you, knowing how much harder
it is to bear anguish of mind than of body. But

it was the crucifixion of her heart which crowned
Mary as Queen of Martyrs.   May she console and
strengthen you !'

   " The greater portion of our converts and cate-
chumens, however, had been able to escape before this
last terrible outburst; and out of those that remained,
we have had but two instances of apostasy—one of a
poor fellow of rather weak intellect, who was put to the
torture for eight days, and who yielded at last; but no
sooner had the fatal assent been wrung from him, than
he gave himself up to positive despair : he spends his
days in crying and going from his own house to the
prison, where our faithful confessors are lying, burning for an opportunity to atone for his weakness.
The other is a *Deftera*, or doctor, who for a fortnight,
in addition to dungeon and chains, received a daily
bastinado.   After which, finding him invincible, they
invented a new method of torture: binding him with a
kind of hard bands, which had been previously dis-
tended by being soaked in water, and which, in drying
and returning to their natural size, cut deeply into the
flesh, so that the blood streamed from the wounds in
every direction.   This torture, prolonged for many
days and nights, at last overcame his powers of endurance, and the poor *Deftera* yielded, though not
without bitter remorse.   The rest, although continually put to the question for the last six weeks, have
remained firm.   At the fourth interrogatory, they

were again offered liberty on condition of their sign-
ing the *Credo.* ' If our legs do not suffice,' was the
heroic answer, ' take our heads; we will never renounce our faith.'

" You will understand that, as for the pastor, so for
his flock, there can be no consolation but in the entire
immolation of ourselves to the Divine will. As for
me, unworthy to share in the sufferings of my beloved spiritual children, my prison is a royal palace,
compared with theirs; and my guards, lambs in comparison with those leopards in human form who, in
their case, as in that of the holy St. Ignatius, add every
species of brutality to the fulfilment of their duty. My
cell is four feet square; and I am given some straw,
which I share with my keepers—a luxury denied to
them. Oh! why have my sins rendered me unworthy of the glorious title of confessor for Christ,
which my brethren have so nobly earned? All I
can do in the depths of my dungeon is, to strive by
my letters and my prayers to console and strengthen
my suffering children, and obtain, if possible, some
alleviation of their tortures. Several times I had
heard of Cassa's being in the habit of paying secret
and unexpected visits to the prisons; and I had resolved, on the very first opportunity, to try and
obtain in this way a personal interview with him.
One day I heard a slight noise at the door of my
cell; and, on running to open it, saw Cassa alone,

without guards and without shoes, going stealthily
into an adjoining cell. I rapidly went over in my
mind the form of the petition I had resolved to
address to him ; but, to my great disappointment,
he left the cell by an opposite door. I had a native
servant, however, who was personally devoted to me,
and who undertook to follow and speak to him. My
object was to implore the release of my poor confessors from the *ghend*, or, if not, the permission to
share it with them. But Cassa was inexorable. He
listened to my messenger with tolerable patience, but
replied : ' They are very well where they are ; let
them suffer the punishment which their own obstinacy
has brought upon them. As for the Abouna Jacobis,
an armed escort shall conduct him to the frontier,
from whence he may return to his own country. The
Abouna Salama detests him. I will have nothing to
say to the matter.' So ended my hopes for my poor
fellow-prisoners. May God's holy will be done !"

In spite of his insatiable desire for martyrdom,
God reserved our holy apostle for a different kind of
confessorship. After many weary months of prison,
Cassa determined to send him, as he had said, to
Sennaar, and there to shut him up in a more inaccessible dungeon, called the Arab fortress. But the
soldiers of his escort, in concert with the governor
of Matamma, touched by the sight of such sanctity
and courage, resolved to disobey their orders, and to

furnish him with the means of escape. Mgr. de Jacobis did not lose a moment in returning to the province of Tigré, and in a few weeks appeared at Halaï. There Cassa heard of him; and at once wrote to the French consul, complaining of the incomparable audacity of Mgr. de Jacobis, and declaring that he would have either the exile or the death of this "incorrigible rebel." Not to compromise the interests of the mission, the poor Bishop was again obliged to abandon his flock, and to take refuge in the burning sand-hills of Massouah. It seemed to him impossible, however, to rejoice in his liberty, while his brethren were still in that terrible Gondar dungeon. One of them, however, was soon to be released by death from his continual sufferings; and the account of his life and martyrdom was given at length by Mgr. de Jacobis in the following letter to the Cardinal Prefect of the Propaganda:

"Abba Ghebra Mikael, our new Abyssinian martyr, was born in the province of Godjam, a peninsula formed by the waters of the Blue Nile, which there takes its source. He studied in various towns of his native country, and there became celebrated for his talents and science. He taught astronomy, medicine, history, and ancient languages; and became, in process of time, the tutor of the late emperor. From Godjam, he went to the province of Tigré, where his reputation had already preceded him, and where he

composed an Ethiopian dictionary which is the one
now in general use.   It was in 1841 that I first became acquainted with him, and found that, unlike the
generality of his countrymen, he had deeply studied
religious questions, and was well read in Gheez, the
language of the sacred books; but had as yet not
joined himself to any particular sect, not having been
satisfied with the contradictions which his clear and
logical mind discovered in the heretical works which
had hitherto been his only study.   He was one of the
Abyssinian deputation sent by King Oubié to Cairo,
and accompanied me to Rome in 1842.   There, all
difficulties having been cleared away, he embraced the
Catholic faith with an ardour and a devotion which
have entitled him to receive the martyr's palm.   On
his return, he openly announced his convictions, and
was in consequence imprisoned for three months by the
Abouna Salama, and only rescued by King Oubié at
the time of his quarrel with that heretical prelate.
From that time, his house became the rendezvous of
all converts, and a kind of class-room for theology,
literature, and every species of useful science.   It is
with his help that I learnt the different dialects of
the country, and with his assistance that I composed
the various catechisms and elementary religious works
which have become the text-books of our native priests
and converts.   His life was entirely devoted to prayer
and to the instruction of his people in the Catholic

faith, for which his great erudition admirably qualified him. Who so fitted, therefore, for the priesthood? It is an intense joy to me to think that I was permitted to confer on him, in 1851, the sacrament of ordination; and, in spite of the humility which had made him think himself unworthy of the office, a holy and remarkable expression of intense happiness and peace showed itself on his face when the ceremony was concluded. Taken prisoners together, at Gondar, on the 15th July 1854, we were rudely separated, in spite of our entreaties, and took leave of each other with tears, though little thinking it was to be for the last time. But during those five months a correspondence was kept up between us, which, if published, would, on his part, compare with the most glorious annals of the Church's martyrs.

"No sooner was he thrown into prison, than his torturers scourged him with such severity that his bones were almost laid bare, and his chest was so bruised that a violent hæmorrhage of the lungs was the result. In fact, the next day it was universally reported that he was dead. One of the younger priests, who had witnessed his sufferings, and had been afterwards thrown into a prison adjoining, called out to him, 'My father, for two days they have given us absolutely nothing—neither bread nor water; and I have heard that this is enough to kill the strongest man in three days. Is there a hope that we may so soon see our Lord?' 'My son,' replied Abba Ghebra Mikael, 'in this dark and terrible dungeon it is impossible to distinguish day from night, and it is almost equally impossible to keep a count of time. I know, however, that, even with a fast like ours, it is possible to live through the octave.' 'In any case, father,' replied the young man, 'the day cannot be far distant when we shall rejoice in the glory of His presence who is eternal life.' The venerable Abba replied, 'Come, then, O good Jesus! come, then, O Bread of Life! my Saviour and my God! come quickly!' Every moment his strength diminished. At last, one day, he fell forward on the broken and disjointed floor of his prison; his head passed through the aperture with part of his body, and then rested on a beam of wood; and he remained for two whole days in this state, with his legs suspended in the air—no one having come to see after or to release him.

"After five months of this horrible imprisonment, he was conducted to Cassa's camp, with these words from the Abouna Salama: 'To-day I shall condemn to the torture of the *giraf* the accursed men calling themselves Catholics, who have been perverted by the French missionaries. Hasten to have the scaffold prepared for the arch-heretic whom I now send you!' *Sic dicit Pharaoh!*

"Brought into the presence of the Emperor and his whole court, he made, with incredible firmness and eloquence, a defence and profession of his faith, the whole camp being witnesses of his boldness and courage. Having triumphed over all the arguments brought against him, he was condemned to be beheaded. But this was too merciful a sentence for the Abouna. He was ordered to receive 150 strokes of the *giraf* on the face. This was done, and he fell on the pavement as one dead. Then the Emperor, as if filled with diabolical fury, exclaimed, ' Send for the stoutest whips of the bullock-drivers of Abyssinia, and let the strongest men among them flog him on the most tender parts of his body, so that he may die. Let there be relays of men, that, when the one set is weary, the others may lash on.' It was then no longer possible to count the strokes which fell on his mangled body, while the martyr repeated, with a loud voice, the magnificent confession of faith of St. Leo, and the declaration of the Council of Chalcedon on the dogma of the two natures of Jesus Christ; until the people cried shame, and the executioners and the Emperor himself were weary of tormenting him.

" But then—O miracle of love and power !—instead of expiring, as Cassa expected, under the torture, the old man rose, bearing on his face no trace of the wounds he had received. This was attested by witnesses too numerous to be doubted. The exasperated Emperor, only the more hardened by this miracle, ordered him back to prison, and to be heavily chained. Two days

after, he was sentenced to follow the army, with irons
on his legs, across a difficult and almost impracticable
road. An English agent arriving the same day, the
order was countermanded, and he was again dragged
before the tribunal, where the Abouna Salama presided.
Subject to a fresh interrogatory, he renewed his profession of faith in the following terms: ' I believe and
I adore in our Lord Jesus Christ our actual human
nature united to the Divine nature in the Person of
the Word; I believe and I confess that the Word was
made flesh, and that there are two natures in one
Person.'

"For this declaration, he was again condemned
to death and dragged to the scaffold. But the multitude, struck more and more by his invincible constancy, interfered to prevent the execution; and the
Emperor, afraid of a serious revolt, remanded him to
prison.

"Here he was put under the charge of an officer,
to prevent his escape, as the Abouna maliciously
represented that the other confessors at Gondar had
done. This officer was secretly a disciple and a great
admirer of our holy martyr, and gave free access to all
who wished to visit or relieve him. In the extreme
destitution to which the camp was reduced from
the continual inroads and surprises of the Gallas
tribe, these timely succours were the means of pro-
longing his life; but, faithful to the charity which

was his characteristic, he reserved scarcely any thing
for himself, distributing the surplus among the poorer
soldiers, and speaking to all words of such encourage-
ment and instruction, that he became, as it were, the
apostle of the camp.

"His sufferings, however, had exhausted his
strength; fearful pains in the stomach came on,
accompanied by dysentery. As it was impossible for
him to walk, they procured him a mule, in spite of
the king's orders, and, when the march began, they
fastened him on to the saddle like an inanimate body.
All this time, his noble dignity, sweetness, and gentleness never forsook him. The soldiers called him no
longer by his own name, but by that of *Quedus
Ghiorghis*—Saint George. This saint, according to
the Abyssinian legend, lost his life seven times for his
faith, and was raised up again seven times to defend
it. It seemed as if God were willing to confirm the
belief of the good soldiers; for it was on the 13th
July, the day set apart in the Abyssinian calendar for
this martyr's feast, that He called His faithful and
valiant soldier home. He died on the march and in
his chains, bearing witness to the last to the truth as
it is in Christ Jesus.

"The rough soldiers wept bitterly at his death,
and gave him honourable burial."

Mgr. de Jacobis afterwards sent a picture of the
martyr to the Superior-General at Paris, with these

words, dated June 29, 1858 : " I send you the portrait
of Abyssinia's first martyr, which represents him so
exactly, that it is quite wonderful to me, knowing the
ignorance of drawing of the person who took the like-
ness ; and also a Latin epitaph, in which I have styled
him ' one of our seminarists.' He was, in reality,
only a postulant ; but in heart and desire he has long
belonged to our Congregation, among whom I feel
sure that his name will be received with the veneration
it deserves." He also preserved an Ethiopian Ms.,
written in Abba Ghebra Mikael's own hand, which is
now in the reliquary of the Mission-house at Paris.

A second letter from Mgr. de Jacobis, written to the
superior of the sisters of charity in Alexandria, who
had tenderly nursed one of the escaped confessors of
Gondar in the terrible illness which was the result of
his captivity, will give us some further details of the
cruelty of the new Emperor.

After thanking her for her kindness and charity
towards the captive, he continues :

" Since the Emperor has imbrued his hands so
largely in innocent blood, it seems as if his good star
had deserted him. His army has been defeated, and
his troops decimated by fever and dysentery. These
reverses seem only to have added spite to his natural
brutality. Among our martyrs was a young and deli-
cate woman, Wozoro Laïm-Laïm, who, after having
given birth to a son in the prison where she was con-

fined, was, by Cassa's orders, flogged to death. In the
midst of her punishment, the executioners tried to take
away her child from her; she remonstrated: 'You
will let him die of want after I am gone—better that he
should suffer for the same faith as his mother, and die
at the same time.' A multitude of others, left for
weeks in the torture of the *ghend*, were only released
to be scourged or bastinadoed, and that with unheard-of severity. The Emperor has, likewise, exasperated his subjects by his treachery. Having King
Oubié in his power, he put him in the front of
the battle which was about to be fought against his
own son. The son, to save his father's life, and on the
solemn promise of the Emperor to give him a safe
conduct, surrendered the disputed pass without a
struggle. Theodoros broke his word, threw the unfortunate prince into prison, and seized upon all his
treasures.

"By a similar act of treachery, he took possession of the mountain of Ghai Chaïn, celebrated for
its valuable library; and carried his barbarity to the
point of skinning the unfortunate *Dejesmac*, or governor,—hanging his skin on a tree to intimidate the
people of the district. His companion, and principal
officer, was hung up by the tongue, the cord passing
through his brain. Others he nailed to the earth—
not through the temples, like Sisera, but piercing
them through the body. All these execrable crimes

have made him the terror of the whole country, so
that he is looked upon as another Nero or Robespierre.

"He has also pillaged and sacked the *Oueros* of
Lasta. These are ten celebrated churches cut in the
solid rock by order of the Emperor Lalibala. Alvarez
affirms this work to be unique in the world, and M.
Montuori made some drawings of it which he took to
Naples. When the news of the destruction of these
magnificent temples became known, the indignation
roused among the clergy against Theodoros knew no
bounds; and now that he has made enemies of the
merchants, whom he has pillaged, and of the husband-
men, whose crops he has destroyed, it is hard to say
to what section he is to turn for help or sympathy
in case of a reverse.

"To crown his iniquities, he has forced the Abouna
Salama to ordain him priest, under the title of *Gian*,
signifying 'the Merciful;' thus endeavouring to unite
in his own person the offices of priest and king. The
Abouna, in spite of his unworthy compliance, has
himself fallen into disgrace. The other day, the
Coptic Patriarch from Cairo, the Abouna Daoud,
arrived unexpectedly in Abyssinia, and began his
pastoral visit by causing the Abouna Salama to be
publicly beaten, and then addressed the Emperor in
terms of violent reproach. Theodoros, in a rage,
desired both the Bishops (whom he called in derision
the 'two Turks') to be seized and shut up in a little

enclosure full of thorns and dried wood, to which he was about to set fire, ' so as to burn them like scorpions,' when, on their promising profound submission to and compliance with his wishes, he released them—after eight days of agonising terror—and commanded them to follow the march of his army. In vain the poor Cairo Patriarch implored permission to return to Egypt. The crafty Abyssinian replied, ' Our chronicles affirm that you are the first Patriarch who has deigned to visit us; I could not, therefore, think of depriving my people of such an honour.' The Protestant missionaries have met with similar treatment. M. Krapf, sent by Bishop Gobat to the Emperor, who had written to say that he would receive him with ' honour and joy,' found himself suddenly seized, imprisoned, and finally driven out of the country, and compelled to take refuge in Malta. All religions share the same fate—at least, all who will not acknowledge the new Emperor as their spiritual head. At the beginning of his reign he had passed a law to abolish slavery; but now we have the melancholy spectacle day by day of seeing hundreds of these poor creatures, most of them boys and girls, driven in gangs to the sea-coast, where they are sold like brute beasts to the highest bidder—so completely has his supposed philanthropy evaporated with his usurpation of supreme power."

In the midst of so much suffering, Mgr. de Jacobis

had the consolation of being still able to exercise his
ministerial functions in the province of Agamié.
After the entire defeat of Oubié and the imprisonment of his son, his nephew Négousié had put himself at the head of the Tigré army, and had succeeded
in stopping the advance of Theodoros towards the
coast of the Red Sea. He determined, likewise, to
claim the assistance of France ; and, for that purpose,
sent an embassy to Paris, imploring the protection of
that country. Négousié loved Mgr. de Jacobis, and
gave him every facility for his missions. Soon after, a
French ship arrived at Massouah, whose commander,
M. Moquet, sent a message to Mgr. de Jacobis,
begging him to come to him without delay on urgent
public affairs, as he (M. Moquet) was detained by illness
on board his ship. Mgr. de Jacobis started at once ;
and, on making the usual evening halt in the desert
of Samahar, went to say his Office in the shade of some
trees, a little way from the rest of his party. All of
a sudden he looked up and saw an enormous lion re-
clining in the adjoining thicket, lying forward on his
paws, and attentively watching him : he was scarcely
three paces off. Mgr. de Jacobis quietly took off his
coarse Abyssinian cloak, and laid it on the ground
between him and the lion, while he slowly and quietly
retraced his steps backwards towards his companions,
always keeping his enemy in sight. The beast gave
a low roar, and evidently longed to follow, but was

deterred by fear of the cloak. Some of Mgr. de
Jacobis' Abyssinian guides wanted to attack him on
the spot, but he dissuaded them from so rash an act,
and said : " We will remain here quietly till morning,
under God's care, and then continue our journey."
The next day, the mangled remains of a large antelope
at the entrance to the thicket showed them how God
had provided a substitute for His faithful servant,
as a reward for his faith. The rest of the journey
was performed without further adventures : but his
humility was put to a severe test when, on his arrival
at Massouah, he was received by a salute of eight
guns, and the most profound respect, by the officers
and sailors of the vessel. M. Moquet had come to
request, in the name of the French Emperor, permission to build a church at Massouah. The answer of
the Pacha being in the negative, M. Moquet proceeded to Djeddah to enforce his request, which was
finally granted. The importance of this concession
arose from the fact that Massouah is looked upon as a
dependency of Mecca, and as yet no Christian church
had ever been allowed to be erected there.

Mgr. de Jacobis had also the satisfaction of seeing
his old friend, M. Stella, who had just arrived from
the Bogos country, and who brought good news from
Mgr. Biancheri. A new church had been erected in
that district; and that of Alitiena had been completed.
It was a handsome building, composed of three aisles,

and was served by a large body of zealous priests, who were reaping a large harvest of souls.

Comforted and strengthened, Mgr. de Jacobis returned to his little mountain mission of Halaï. But a succession of untoward events in the following year deprived him of this his last resting-place, and cut short a life so valuable to this distracted country.

We have before mentioned the embassy sent by Négousié to Paris. It was favourably received; and the following year M. de Russel was sent by the French government to establish relations with the new King of the Tigré, and to endeavour to come to some arrangement as to establishing a port on the Red Sea; as well as to insure liberty of conscience to the people under his dominion. M. de Russel arrived, however, at an unfavourable moment. Négousié had been defeated by the Emperor's troops; and, whether from fear of consequences or from excess of prudence, refused to see M. de Russel, or to receive his letters. The account of this unfortunate expedition—resulting, as it did, in a second imprisonment of our holy Bishop—is given in a letter from M. Delmonte (dated the 6th of February 1860),—who had been sent to assist Mgr. de Jacobis,—and who writes to the Superior-General as follows:

"On the 12th of January I arrived at Halaï. On going into the house, I perceived a little old man sitting on the ground at the door, wrapped in a

kouari, or common white Abyssinian cloak, reading
a book: he might have been taken for a beggar.
This was Mgr. de Jacobis. On seeing me, he sprang
up; and we remained silent for a few moments, with
our hearts too full to speak; as for me, I could
not help crying for joy. He made me every kind of
excuse for his inability to give me a room, or even a
chair, as the whole house was occupied by M. de
Russel and his suite. Seeing, however, my venerable
Bishop perfectly contented without any accommodation
whatever, I felt only too happy to share in his privations.

"This embassy has been a failure. The king,
Négousié, had been obliged to retreat to the mountain-
fastnesses of Sémien, where alone he and his army
were safe from the pursuit of the Emperor's troops. A
civil war had burst out on all sides; and M. de Russel
was not only unable to continue his route, but pre-
cluded from the possibility of returning to the sea-
shore. On the 6th of February, at four o'clock in the
afternoon, one of Theodoros's generals, named Zaraï,
came to request M. de Russel's presence at the Emperor's court, saying that he had been commanded to
conduct him thither. M. de Russel refused. The next
day the whole village was swarming with armed men;
so that we were, virtually, prisoners in our own house.
M. de Russel armed his officers and men; but forbade
their firing without orders. This was a very necessary precaution; as, had a drop of blood been spilt,

the whole of us would have been mercilessly sacrificed.
Zaraï then sent a second message to M. de Russel,
threatening him with serious consequences in the event
of his continued refusal.* M. de Russel replied simply,
that he had nothing to do with the Emperor, and had no
mission to him or to his court; and that, if he wanted
to see him, he had a sufficient escort without the
troops of Zaraï. The general, incensed at this continued refusal, ordered his men to attack the house.
Affairs were getting serious, when Mgr. de Jacobis
came forward as mediator. He knew Zaraï well, having frequently lodged in his house; and he therefore
asked for a conference, which was granted. Zaraï
countermanded the assault; and, towards nine in the
evening, came with two of his aides-de-camp, and,
after three profound obeisances, sat himself on a
carpet by the Bishop's side. Zaraï explained that he
had received the Emperor's orders to prevent the
French embassy from leaving Halaï; and that, understanding they were about to do so, he had no
alternative but to obey his master. After a long conference, Zaraï said that, if Mgr. de Jacobis would give
himself up as hostage, and take upon himself the re-
sponsibility of the return of M. de Russel and his suite
to Massouah, he (Zaraï) would evacuate the place,
and leave them in peace. To this Monsignor agreed;
and they parted soon after midnight on this pacific
understanding.

"The next morning, however, Zaraï, in defiance
of his word, threatened to burn down the house if M.
de Russel would not accompany him to the Emperor's
camp. His own troops, indignant at his treachery,
refused to obey his orders. Then Zaraï exacted a
renewal of Monsignor's promise; which he, to our
great reluctance and sorrow, gave.. Zaraï pretended
to have received instructions to this effect from the
Emperor himself; but, when we asked to see his
credentials, there was no mention whatever of the
embassy in them. M. de Russel wrote then to the
Emperor Theodoros, to ask him what were his inten-
tions, promising to wait at Halaï for his answer. The
Emperor, however, had by that time left Adoua, and
returned to the central provinces of Abyssinia; so
that a reply would have prolonged M. de Russel's stay
almost indefinitely. The French ambassador, therefore, determined to escape secretly by night on the
8th of the month. He found that the French consul
had sent to the foot of the mountains of Taranta—
which were about four hours' journey from Halaï—
a body of soldiers, under the command of Naib—one
of the chiefs of the Choho tribe—who would conduct
him in safety on board the *Yeman*, which was anchored
in the port of Massouah. M. de Russel communicated
his intention to the Bishop, who discussed the question
calmly and quietly, giving the reasons for and against,
but never alluding to the way in which this sudden

departure might compromise him after his having pledged his word for the ambassador. The latter, however, fearful of another attack, persisted in escaping as he had proposed. He started at midnight on foot,—accompanied by one of the chiefs of Taconda,— and arrived safely on the other side of the mountains of Taranta, where he found the promised troops, who escorted him to Massouah.

" No sooner had the day dawned at Halaï, however, than the peasants came to know if the French ambassador were still there. When they found he was gone, they gave the signal of alarm. We were all praying in the cold and damp little mission-chapel, and Monsignor had just vested for Mass. In a few moments the chapel was thronged with an angry mob, and the Bishop felt it would be no longer prudent to continue the holy Sacrifice. Having finished the Epistle, he left the altar, took off his robes, quietly drank a cup of coffee, and then presented himself calmly and courageously to the people who sought his life. Without giving him time to make the smallest preparation, or to take any thing with him, they carried him off, first to Taconda, and then to Eneto, a day's journey from here. By having pledged himself for the French ambassador, he was irretrievably compromised, and there was nothing to be done. The people will only release him, they say, on the order of the Emperor; and God knows how little likely that will be when he finds him once more in his power. I implored permission to accompany him, but he quietly and decidedly told me to remain and take his place. It was all he had time to say before his departure. I could only follow him with my tears and prayers. Two young native monks insisted on going with him, which was some consolation to me, as I felt they might, perhaps, be able to have access to him in his captivity. When I had lost sight of the melancholy procession, I could only go back into the house and weep bitterly. Some of the native clergy gave me hopes that with money I might be able to contrive his escape. I wrote instantly to M. de Russel to tell him what had happened, and ask for help. He replied by saying that he would directly place 100 talaris at the disposal of the consul at Massouah, expressing his deep sorrow at having been the cause of this great misfortune, and imploring me to leave no stone unturned to obtain Mgr. de Jacobis' release. I wrote also to our holy Bishop; and obtained a few lines in pencil from him, which ran as follows :

" ' Eneto, February 9, 1860.

" ' DEAREST BROTHER,—Benedictus Deus, qui consolatur nos in omni tribulatione nostrâ.

" ' Your letter, so full of love and charity, would have comforted me even had they thrown me into a den of lions. But I am, on the contrary, lodged

with the mules and the cows; in fact, I am only too
well treated. You have full authority from me as to
all which concerns the mission, and there is nothing
to fear now that I am out of the way. I send you all
my blessing, especially to the good Brother Filippini.
I have given him permission to go to Emkoullou; he
can start when he pleases. I recommend myself
specially to your prayers and to those of our dear
students and children; and remain, in the Heart of
Jesus and Mary, your devotedly affectionate,

" ' J. DE JACOBIS.'

"This letter touched me inexpressibly. I could
only commend him, with all my heart, to the Divine mercy, and leave all things to His adorable
will.

"15th Feb. By a decision of the tribes, Monsignor has been to-day brought back to Taconda,
where I fear he is in the hands of some of the agents
of the Abouna Salama. But we are moving heaven
and earth for his deliverance.

"20th March. By the mercy of God, his release has
been accomplished. Through a judicious application
of the money sent by the French consul, the monks
contrived to gain the three chiefs of Halaï and
Taconda. This affair was managed without the knowledge of Mgr. de Jacobis, who wrote to me on the
2d, imploring me to take refuge in Massouah, as he

understood that a plot had been organised to seize and drag me before Theodoros. This letter was brought to me by one of the chiefs whom he had bought, and who told me that he had profited by the rumour of the approaching arrival of the Emperor to persuade the people to send Mgr. de Jacobis to Emkoullou. His patience and holiness had so won upon their affections, that they would all have taken up arms sooner than let him fall into his enemy's hands. Finding that they were determined to defend him by force, and to avoid the effusion of blood, Mgr. de Jacobis at last consented to make his escape, but on condition that, should Theodoros claim the fulfilment of his pledge, he should be permitted to return. Every preparation was secretly made for his departure, and at midnight he started, with one monk ; the other was to remain and keep watch, as usual, at his door, that his departure might not be suspected. We, in the mean while, left Halaï the night before, dividing ourselves into four separate bodies, and taking different routes, that our movements might not excite suspicion. In my intense anxiety to see Monsignor, I took the shortest, though the most dangerous path, with two monks and one of our children. We arrived safely at Emkoullou on the 6th, about four o'clock in the morning ; and there I had the joy of finding Mgr. Biancheri, who had come to fetch various things necessary for his mission, and whom the disturbed state of the country had compelled to remain till the hostile bands which now ravaged it had dispersed.

"Six hours after, Mgr. de Jacobis appeared. You may guess our joy and thankfulness. We all threw ourselves at his feet; he would not suffer that; but raised and embraced us, exclaiming, 'Let us bless our good God, who has united us once more in safety and peace.' As for him, he was frightfully altered and emaciated. He owned to having travelled on foot for two days and nights without stopping; and we heard from the young monk, that at Taconda he had fallen ill and could digest nothing, that it was impossible to procure for him the kind of food which his state rendered necessary, and that the privations of his captivity had terribly undermined his health. If he has suffered thus for twenty-two days, it has been entirely to save M. de Russel and the honour of France, of which I hope that nation will be aware. As for myself, I was so exhausted by fatigue and anxiety that I could scarcely answer his inquiries as to our Halaï mission; and, after renewing our thanks to Him who had so mercifully spared His holy servant, we separated, to take the rest we all so greatly needed."

CHAPTER IX.

The death of Monsignor de Jacobis.

ST. VINCENT DE PAUL, speaking one day to his missionaries, and talking of charity to our neighbour, exclaimed, " If some one were to find a poor missionary, exhausted with want and fatigue, dying under a hedge, and were to ask him, ' What has reduced you to such an extremity?' what joy, my brethren, to be able to answer, ' It is *love* which has done this—the love of our Lord, the love of the souls for which He gave His precious Blood!' Oh, how would this poor missionary, despised of men, be esteemed by God and His holy angels!" St. Vincent must have thought of these words when, from the height of his glory, he witnessed this very sight in the person of our holy and saint-like Bishop.

As we have already related, his last imprisonment had completely exhausted his strength; added to which, the exchange from the reviving air of the mountains to the insufferable heat of the plains at that season, acting on a frame already so enfeebled by the sufferings and privations of a twenty years' apostolate, completed the sacrifice of the life which he had so freely offered for his Abyssinian children.   Four

months after his last escape from prison, Mgr. de
Jacobis went home to receive his reward.

The following account of his death is from the pen
of M. Delmonte:

"Emkoullou, August 3, 1860.

"I have to announce to you the death of a saint:
Mgr. de Jacobis gave up his pure spirit to God on
the 31st of July 1860, at half-past three o'clock in
the afternoon. Ever since the 19th of July he foresaw that his end was at hand. He would fain have
died a martyr, like Abba Ghebra Mikael; but God
reserved to him a slower and, perhaps, a more painful
martyrdom, though one equally precious to the eye
of faith. A raging fever, which on the 19th of July
produced several hours of violent delirium, was to him
an evident sign that God was about to call him to Himself. Feeling that his fever never left him but for a
few hours in the middle of the day, and that most of
the monks who had accompanied him were equally
suffering, he resolved to return to Halaï, where, the
rainy and cooler season having set in, there was more
hope that the invalids might recover their strength.
I represented to him the difficulties of the road, the
excessive heat, and his own extreme weakness; for
he had eaten nothing for seven days. But he always
replied, 'that it was the will of God that he should go.'
He left Emkoullou, therefore, on the 29th July, at half-
past five in the afternoon, taking with him all the

Halaï monks, and about ten children of our schools who were being trained for the ministry. I was compelled to remain behind, with two of the monks, to overlook some repairs which were being made to the church and house, and which Monsignor was very anxious should be completed before the rainy season set in during the following month.

"After five hours' march, Monsignor arrived at Arkiko, where the brother of the Naib Adris was waiting to offer him hospitality for the night. Monsignor thankfully accepted it, and got some sleep; but the fever returned with great violence, and did not leave him till three in the morning. Towards four o'clock he resumed his march. They traversed the plain of Kattra, he reciting the morning prayers, and giving his usual instruction, only saying with more than common earnestness: 'Pray, my children! pray! for prayer is the nourishment of the soul, and fortifies the body. Pray! for I feel I greatly need your prayers.'

"They arrived at noon at the valley of Zarayé, where he asked for a little bread, which was given to him. As he had eaten nothing for so many days, his companions were rejoiced, and thought it a sign of returning health. At Sahto he drank a little fresh water, which seemed to revive him greatly. The night was passed at Hidelik. Here the fever returned with such force that he was again delirious for four

hours. This did not prevent, however, his resuming
the usual march of the caravan two hours before sun-
rise. For the next three hours he did not speak. At
last, he said to those nearest him: ' My children, let
us go slowly; for I feel my strength decreasing, and
that my head will bear no more.' This was at ten
o'clock in the morning, when the sun had become
almost overpowering. This portion of the road is the
most painful and wearisome of the whole, especially
during the hot season; for it is through a long and
very narrow valley, bounded on both sides by arid
and high mountains, which reflect the intense heat of
the sun, and the very sight of which startles one by
the rugged and precipitous appearance of their peaks,
which look as if they would fall over and crush the
passers-by in the narrow gorge below. The air was
like that out of the mouth of a furnace; the earth
positively burnt one's feet; and even the camels were
with difficulty persuaded to go on.

"Monsignor was now completely exhausted. Arrived at Alghédien at eleven o'clock in the morning, he was compelled to stop, no longer being able to
sit his mule. He sat down on a stone, looking at the
sky, and from time to time drawing long sighs. Then
he wrapped his *natlah* round his head,—which is a
species of cloak that is worn by the Abyssinian monks
during the summer,—and thus they hoped that he
slept. But he was only preparing himself for the last

great struggle. Then he lifted his head, which he had
leant forward on his knees, and asked for a confessor
and a last absolution. This done, he called around
him all his monks, and, with surprising strength of
voice, made them a touching parting exhortation, re-
commending to them perseverance in their holy vocation, charity to one another, zeal for souls, obedience
to all orders proceeding from Rome (that is, from the
Pope, as the successor of St. Peter, and the Vicar of
our Lord), and submission to all Bishops and priests
sent by him to their country. Then he gave them a
solemn benediction; and all answered in their language : '*Amien, abtacten! amien !*'—' Amen, beloved
father! amen!' At the same moment, all the monks,
children, and even Mahometans, burst into tears,
smiting their breasts, and kissing his feet and hands.
Monsignor then begged for Extreme Unction. The
holy oils were brought. He stretched himself on the
burning earth, with only a stone for his pillow, and
thus received the Sacrament of the Dying. He
evidently suffered terribly; but his face was calm,
and he repeated in Ethiopian the responses to all the
prayers which the native priest was pronouncing over
him. After that, to the distress and astonishment of
all, he raised himself on his knees, and, in that posture,
humbly asked pardon of all present for the scandal he
said he had given them by his life and example during
the time he had spent among them. He declared

o

himself the most miserable of sinners, and that his
only hope was in the merits of our Saviour, and in
the intercession of the Mother of God and of St.
Vincent de Paul; affirming that it was only through
His sufferings, and by the help of their prayers, that
he trusted to be accepted by God, before whom he
was about, in a few minutes, to appear. All present
burst into tears. He sat himself again on the stone,
and leant his head against the rock which was on his
left. A little mimosa-tree—a specimen of the *spina
Christi*—sheltered him slightly from the burning sun.
They thought all was over; but it was not so. After
a few moments he again opened his eyes. 'Pray for
me, my children,' he murmured; 'for I am dying.
I shall not forget you; I will pray for you always;
pray for me. God bless you all!'

"Again he leant his dear and venerable head against
the rock ; that head which had never rested in its
labours for souls : and then, covering his face with his
natlah, he quietly slept in our Lord.

"Thus did Abyssinia's great apostle finish his
earthly pilgrimage, in the sixtieth year of his age, and
the twenty-first of his apostolate in Ethiopia. It is
almost impossible for me to describe to you the
sorrow of the people of all classes and of all creeds—
Catholics, Mussulmans, schismatics—all alike, with
tears in their eyes and ashes on their heads, go on
crying out, 'Our father is dead!' 'That blessed

one!' 'That saint of God!' The heat is still excessive. Réaumur's thermometer marks 38° in the shade. The monks who accompanied our holy Bishop are in the greatest despair: one of them has died at the same spot as Mgr. de Jacobis. All are doing their utmost to hasten their march, so as to carry his remains to Evo, a Catholic mission where he wished to be interred. In spite of the heat, I am going to start to-morrow for that place."

"Evo, 11th September 1860.

"I continue my letter of the 3d of August. Having received the necessary instructions from Mgr. Biancheri, I started with my Ethiopian interpreter, and one guide, a highway-robber by profession, but on whom I could rely; for he had accompanied Mgr. de Jacobis, and was personally devoted to him. After sunset, we halted in a valley named Zaragi. A tropical rain, which began at nine in the evening, and fell in torrents till seven in the morning, gave us no chance of a moment's rest; we had no umbrella, and there was neither a rock nor a tree which would afford the smallest shelter. Neither could we continue on our road, on account of the pitchy darkness. It was a terrible night. The little river, swollen to a torrent, barred our path for five hours; but at last we reached the fatal valley of Alghédien, where our beloved father had breathed his last. My guide, who had

been with him, gave me all the sad details as we
approached each spot. 'Here,' he exclaimed, striking with his stick a large stone,—'Here our holy
Abouna Jacob sat down for the first time, when he
felt his end was at hand. Here he assembled his
monks and children, and spoke to them words of
counsel, humility, and love. This is where he afterwards lay; and here is the stone on which he leant his
head when one of the monks anointed his mouth, and
eyes, and ears, and nostrils, and hands, and feet, with
the holy oils. Then he sat down again on this stone;
and there, wrapped in his cloak, slept the sleep of the
just.' And so saying, my guide, kneeling on the
ground, burst into a violent flood of tears. This man
was a Mahometan, a robber by choice and profession;
yet his heart had been completely melted by our holy
Bishop's words and death.

"After joining my tears with his, I asked him if
he could point out to me where the monk had been
buried who had died a few minutes after Monsignor.
'There,' he replied, pointing to a heap of stones about
twenty yards off. I ran to the spot, for the burning
sun at that hour (two o'clock in the day) did not
admit of any lingering on that broiling sand. I sprang
back in horror. The wild beasts, unable to remove
the stones which covered the grave, had dug a hole at
the side, into which they had dragged the body of the
poor monk, which was almost entirely devoured: only

a portion of the head remained, on which were the marks of their terrible claws. His clothes were torn in pieces, and vermin filled the remaining space. Hastily covering these sad remains with sand, I continued my route, and on the 20th of August arrived at Evo, where I could at last kneel by the grave of my much-loved and venerable Bishop. They had not buried him in the church, but outside, near the wall of the high Altar, as the building itself was so small. I said nothing at the time; but knowing that there were some skilful masons among the monks, I persuaded them to enlarge the church by fifteen feet, and, by knocking down the wall on the Gospel side of the Altar, to bring the grave within the enclosure of the church, where these precious remains would be safer, and more free from the vicissitudes of climate. This done, I returned to the work he had left me, heart-broken at the irreparable loss we had sustained, and yet thankful that he had at last reaped the reward of a life unequalled in devotion, self-sacrifice, and humility; and which has left us an example that may kindle a like zeal for souls in the hearts of others, and bear fruit a hundredfold in this land of his adoption and of his martyrdom."

M. Delmonte writes again on the 13th September 1864:

" I have been again summoned to Evo, by desire of Monsignor Biancheri, to see to the removal

of the remains of our beloved Bishop from their old
tomb to that erected in the new church which has
just been built in this district, the old one being
threatened with instant destruction. This ceremony
was performed on the 10th of July, in presence of
the whole town. I found the coffin almost entirely
destroyed by the white ants ; but the tanned cow-
skin, in which the body of our venerable father had
been wrapped, was intact, and the ligatures which
bound it were equally fresh. One could have imagined that the body was that of one just dead.
Two of the monks and myself lifted the precious
burden from the coffin, and placed it in the middle
of the old church. At this sight, the cries and
lamentations of the people burst forth ; so much so,
that I never could have imagined any thing like it.
All of them—men, women, and children, priests and
monks—threw themselves on the ground, sobbing
aloud, and crying out, ' My father, my father! hear
your poor suppliant children !' I could do nothing but
cry like a child myself. After half an hour spent in this
way, I induced them to follow me in a short prayer,
and then to leave the church to me and two or three
of the monks and men of the place. I then undid the
links which bound the cow-skin round the venerable
body, and found it intact and in perfect preserva-
tion. The hair remained on the head, as well as the
beard on the chin. I reënclosed these sacred remains,

placing them in a new coffin, and put it in a kind of mortuary chapel adjoining the church ; where the inhabitants watched it alternately day and night, until the arrival of Mgr. Biancheri ; who, having certified as to the authenticity of the relics, fixed his seal at the four corners, and then deposited the coffin in the place destined for its reception."

Thus rest the mortal remains of Monsignor de Jacobis, in the place which witnessed the last act of his life of heroic charity ; surrounded by the people for whom he had laboured unto death, and upwards of 25,000 of whom he had brought into the fold of Christ.

All revere him as a saint, come long distances to pray at his tomb, and attribute to his intercession the special mercies they receive. The light of his virtues has dispelled the cloud of error and prejudice which obscured the minds of the Abyssinians.

His name has become a household word among the people ; and even his old enemy, the Emperor Theodoros, when forbidding on a recent occasion the entry of Protestant Bibles into his kingdom, gave as his reason : " We have no need of your sacred books ; for we have those of the Abouna Jacob, who taught us better than any one else the way of salvation." Whilst his fame is extending throughout Abyssinia, that of his persecutors is equally on the decline. The Abouna Salama, his arch-enemy, has been publicly disgraced and imprisoned.* On his imploring. the Emperor to allow him to return to Cairo, he was met by the retort : " No, no ; you have cost us too dear ! Pay back the 20,000 francs you cost us originally, and then we may think about giving you your liberty." All those, in fact, who were instrumental in persecuting the good Bishop, have met with sudden and violent deaths or misfortunes ; while the seed he has sown is bearing fruit a hundredfold ; and the souls he has won are following in his steps, and will hereafter be his glory and his crown.

* While this little book was going through the press, the news was received in Europe of the death of this cruel persecutor, in his dungeon.

THE END.

www.ingramcontent.com/pod-product-compliance
Lightning Source LLC
Chambersburg PA
CBHW020620030726
47497CB00007B/2332